God is Calling Me?!?!?

By Cathy Meyer

First Printing – August 2025

ISBN 978-1-962929-51-6

Proudly Printed in the United States of America
Digital Publishing of Florida, Inc.
Oldsmar, FL 34677

With all this going for us, my dear, dear friends, stand your ground. And don't hold back. Throw yourselves into the work of the Master, confident that nothing you do for Him is a waste of time or effort.

1 Corinthians 15:58 (The Msg)

Table of Contents

Acknowledgements

Gratitude is a word that is often left unexpressed by most people. It is *a state of being thankful of something or to someone.* Experiencing or showing gratitude is an important part in our journey with Christ. Rather or not we are feeling it at the moment, we are to always try and not forget to whom we owe it to and why.

I Love the Lord, not only for His gift of salvation to me, but what He has given me over the years and *not given* me. **John F. Kennedy** said it best;

"As we express our gratitude, we must never forget that the highest appreciation is not to utter words, but to live by them."

That my friends is my goal. To try and live the way Jesus wants and to treat people with the same attitude as He did. That is hard I know, but a goal.

So I sit here and think about how grateful I am to my Lord and Savior for giving me a second chance each and every day to begin again.

I also want to thank and show my appreciation to my Husband Bill, my best friend, whom without a doubt if God had not brought him into my life when He did, I don't know where life would have taken me. I do know it would have been miserable. God brought him into my life at a very early age and the impact that he's had on me has helped to shape my identity and my values. I love and appreciate you Bill.

Introduction

Welcome to God is Calling Me?!?!?

We are going to go on a little journey, hopefully we will discover where we as Christ followers fit into His plans. I'm so excited to begin this journey with you and hopefully this will get us out of our shells and journey into a new and exciting life that Jesus has for us!

There are many women and children in the Bible that are a great example of God using them for His good. We are going to learn about some whom God called into service and how they responded and the result of that calling.

We live in a world that isn't our home, and we are here only for a little while. God sent his people into a foreign land that worshiped foreign gods. Joshua reminded them to not forget who they served. Don't get so caught up in what you are doing and forget who you're doing it for.

You don't have to be afraid; I'm right here with you and my story is a hoot! Hopefully by reading my journey as well as these special individuals you'll see how Good God is and how His patience goes on forever. He doesn't want us to stay where we are, He will gently nudge us toward His purpose for us. He will not force us into anything we are not willing to do though.

Trust me when I say that God's purpose will be done. If we are unwilling to do it, He will get someone else to get the job done. Please never miss an opportunity to be used by God. Trust me when I tell you, you will miss out on one of the greatest blessings God has for you!

So dust off your Bible and get that coffee and let's get started!

Chapter 1

You want me to do what?

I remember as a young wife and mother I felt so out of my league when it came to interacting with those that I felt were above me and my background. My family and I was invited to the grand opening of a church that was new, and I was terrified to say the least. My Aunt pushed me into going. The building was old and needed a lot of work done to it, mostly cosmetics. Well one Sunday after church the Pastor and his wife asked me if I'd have time and would I be willing to help wallpaper the nursery. I said sure I could help, not realizing until it was too late that I had no idea how to wallpaper anything!

Back then they didn't have Google or YouTube to help me. So I did what I thought was best and called a friend whom I knew would know what she was doing and begged her to come that Saturday and help me, so I wouldn't look like an Idiot! Remember when I said I am a lot like Peter? Well this is one of those times! After explaining that I volunteered to do it, She reluctantly said yes and so we went that weekend. My friend knew my secret and the whole time I'm pretending to know what I'm doing, she is laughing at me and giving me looks that said as much.

The thing is, looking back now at the whole thing, I know now that they were trying to get to know me and witness to me. It wasn't long after that that I got saved. I didn't know I needed to repent of my sins, until I did. They were showing me the love of Christ, and I soon became a committed follower of Jesus.

At the time I felt like such a fraud I was lying to the Pastor and his wife! In Church!! Well, after that debacle I'd like to say that I was never quick in volunteering for anything again. I would like to be able to tell you that I learned a valuable lesson that day, but nope, not me.

The Pastor and his wife came to me and another lady after church one Sunday and asked us to help with teaching the k-5 children, again I said yes, I was one of those people who could not say no to others even though I was terrified! I didn't know the Bible, and I sure wasn't smart enough to teach! I didn't have a degree in anything! I went home with the material they had provided to me and studied daily. I felt like such a fraud. I never said no, even though I felt I was the most unqualified of anyone.

Well let me tell you, *that was and is the most rewarding of anything I would and will ever do as a Christ follower.* I not only taught the little ones, but I was learning right along with them!

Because I had to know the lessons to which I was teaching, I was learning God's Word, and all about His love and what His desire for me is. We had a memory verse each week and I had to come up with ways for the kids to memorize them. I was able to, *with the Lord's help*, memorize the scripture and show the kids how easy it was to do. God is so good; He was bringing me to a place where He wanted me to be. Like Moses in **Exodus chapters 2-6.** To make a long story *kind* of short;

Moses was adopted. He was living in a palace! He was I'd say living his best life. He was comfortable in his home, had all the comforts afforded to him. When Moses was 40 years old, Moses ran away, after he killed a man and then lived in the wilderness and became a shepherd. Talk about going from prince to pauper! His life changed dramatically. Then while minding his own business for forty years, God calls to him in a burning bush and after some debating, **Exodus 3: 11** Moses said to God, ***"Who am I, that I should go to Pharaoh to bring the Israelites out of Egypt?"*** and then again in **verses 10-12 of chapter** 4 he says, ***"O Lord, I never have been eloquent, neither in the past nor since you have spoken to your servant. I am slow of speech and tongue."*** The Lord asked him, ***"Who gave man his mouth? Who makes him deaf or mute? Who gives him sight or makes him blind? Is it not I the Lord? Now go; I will help you speak and teach you what to say."*** Eventually Moses, reluctantly does what God asks of him. He was called out of his comfort zone. Like Moses so was I.

I am not a person who likes to try new things especially if it is something out of my comfort zone! But my friend When God calls us, He never leaves it to us to figure out on our own, He prepares us beforehand. If you are being called to do something for the Lord, look back and see where God was preparing you, because He never sends us empty handed. He gave Moses a staff and He also sent Moses' brother Aaron to be his helper. He was preparing Moses for a most difficult and challenging task God needed Him to do. And my friends, it would last forty years.

Now before Moses became Moses....

The Israelites were, in **Exodus 1** according to the Pharaoh, becoming too numerous and he was afraid of them. He said if their enemies started a war the Israelites would join them. The King hatched a plan to minimize the population. He enlisted the help from a couple of midwives who names were *Shiphrah,* and *Puah.* He told them that whenever a male child was born to a Hebrew woman they were to kill it. Well he was talking to the wrong women. They were Hebrew! They were committed to helping the babies, not to harm them. The midwives cared for the babies until the mother was strong enough to. They feared God more than they did the King. They did not kill the male babies, so when asked why baby boys were still being born, They told the king in verse **19 of chapter 1**: *"the Hebrew women are very vigorous and give birth before the midwives arrive."*

The Bible says that God was kind to the midwives and blessed them. The Israelites increased even more, Because these ladies were obedient to God, they were blessed with families of their own. God protected as well as rewarded them. I can imagine the ladies had to be terrified of the King and knowing what could happen to them for disobeying, but they trusted God to take care of the situation.

Now they did lie to the King, but God's law outweighed the Kings. God did not bless the women for lying but for being obedient to Him.

The anger of the Pharoah was so that he then decided to have the baby boys thrown into the Nile river and drowned. Now a Levite woman gave birth to a son and hid him for three months and when she could not hide him any longer she put him in a basket and set him in the reeds along the Nile river. But he floated off. **Exodus 2:4** says: ***His sister stood at a distance to see what would happen to him***. This little girl's name was *Miriam,* she was the older sister of this baby boy, according to what I've been able to dig up on Miriam she was approximately seven years older than Moses. I can picture the little girl wondering what would happen to her brother and I know that She has at this point followed the basket and saw that the daughter of Pharoah found the basket with her brother in it and decided to take him for her own. Miriam seeing this, boldly went up to the princess and asked **in verse 7: *"Shall I go get one of the Hebrew women to nurse the baby for you?"*** The Princess agreed, And Miriam went and got her mother to care for the baby!

Miriam was very brave! Talk about a babysitting Job! The Bible doesn't say if she was scared or if the Princess was suspicious or if Miriam's mother told her to do those things. But the little girl acted and because of her bravery

Moses lived and lead the people out of slavery. God used a little girl to help save His people!

Miriam grew up and when Moses came back after the Israelites she and their other brother Aaron helped Moses bring the people out of Egypt. Aaron was a priest while Miriam was a Prophetess and they along with Moses sang to the LORD for saving them.

Miriam lead the women in song after they had crossed the sea on dry ground.

Numbers 15:21

"Sing to the LORD,

for He is highly exalted.

The Horse and it's rider

He has hurled into the sea."

Well, as all family sagas go, people become jealous of each other for this that and the other. Well, Miriam and Aaron were no different. The Bible says that they began to complain to each other regarding Moses's wife Zipporah. They became envious and prideful over Moses leadership and said In **Numbers 12:2** *: "Has the LORD spoken only through Moses?" Hasn't He also spoken through us?"*

The LORD heard this, and He told Moses, Aaron, and Miriam to come out of the Tent of Meeting. They went out and the LORD came down In a cloud and spoke to them, **Numbers 12:6-8** He said, *"listen to my words:*

When a Prophet of the LORD is among you, I reveal myself to him in visions

I speak to him in dreams, But this is not true of my servant Moses; He is faithful in all my house. With him I speak face to face, Clearly and not in riddles;

He sees the form of the LORD. Why then were you not afraid To speak against my servant Moses?"

The anger of the LORD was such that after He left them and the cloud lifted, Miriam was Leprous. When Aaron saw his sister he begged Moses to not let her remain in that condition. Moses cried out to God and said:

"O' God please heal her!" **verse 13**. Miriam ended up having leprosy for a week then was allowed to return to camp. That my friend is mercy! He could have left her that way permanently, but He didn't. The Lord answered the prayer of Moses because Moses was obedient! He did it for him, not Miriam. His love for us is so that He always watches out for His children. You and I are His Children according to **Romans 8:14-17**. Much like the Israelites who wondered in the desert, we to are wonderers on this earth awaiting for the promised land. But we must remain obedient or live with the consequences of our choices.

God used her to further His kingdom, but He also used her as an example. As a reminder to not criticize or gossip about others because the consequences can be costly.

Miriam made mistakes; as we all do, but the LORD was and is merciful and gracious. He will forgive us and hopefully we will have learned a valuable lesson.

God used her strengths to help Him lead the people and He used her weaknesses as a life lesson on what not to do.

We all can relate to her in many ways. Like for instance; the desert was hot; they walked and walked and walked and walked! Women can be very emotional people. I know I can be. I imagine that she was hot, tired, and grumpy. I know I would be. I mean the woman was in her eighties at this point! I think maybe that the women came up to her and did a lot of whining and complaining. The Bible doesn't elaborate on it. That is just from my experience and from a woman's point of view, as I am currently going through menopause. I do know that she was a quick thinker and a good leader.

I wish I could sit here and tell you with all sincerity that I am a quick thinker, but not me. I remember in my early days as a Christ follower that I met some special women who were walking with the Lord and was a great influence on me and my walk. But I also met some women whom I thought were going to be a great influence and mentor for my walk but ended up being a bad and negative influence.

One such time was when the leadership within the church had changed. I met a woman who was the wife of one of the leaders and I wanted to be friends with her. She seemed so smart and eloquent, and I being a young Christian thought I could learn so much from her. I had at the time been friends with another woman in the church for a few years, that I admired and hung out with at times. Well one day as I was having lunch with the new leaderships wife, she began to degrade and gossip about my other friend, me being me, if you read my book *"Shut My Mouth O'Lord"* you will know what I'm talking about. I preceded to go along with the gossip about my friend, I don't recall what was said, but it had me feeling guilty and I realized that the wife of the leadership in the church was not being a good influence. I feel that she was being used by satan to divide the ladies in the church. I felt so bad that I ended up inviting my friend over for lunch and confessing to her what was said. I cried and asked her to forgive me. She cried and gave me a hug and got up and left. She also left the church! She never spoke to me after that. I lost a good friend over the pettiness of another. **Proverbs 16:28** says; ***"A perverse person stirs up conflict, and a gossip separates close friends."***

John F. Kennedy said: ***"What would it be like if what we said over our lifetime were to be played back for all to hear?"*** That makes you think doesn't it? This reminds me about what Jesus said when speaking to the Pharisees, He said that what we say comes from the heart. **Luke 6:45** says; ***A good man out of the good treasure of his heart brings forth good; and an evil man out of evil treasure of his heart brings forth***

evil. **For out of the abundance of the heart his mouth speaks.** We cannot fix our heart problem by just cleaning up our speech. We must have a *change* of heart. We must ask the Holy Spirit to change us from the inside, then and only then can we begin to change our speech. Jesus has forgiven me this I know. And I on the other hand am learning to watch what I say, and I do my best to think before I speak. And I have learned to choose my friends wisely. It's because of my relationship with Jesus I can do these things. I want to serve Him and please Him. Remember, Just because someone claims to be a Christian doesn't make it so. So choose your influences wisely.

Remember, We need to look inside and think about our motives and what the outcome will be before we open our mouths to criticize someone. Ask yourself, *is it true? Is it kind? Is it necessary?* **Matthew 12:36** says, *"But I tell you that everyone will have to give an account on the day of judgement for every empty word they have spoken."*

That my friends is hard to hear if you only look at the words and not the context. Jesus was saying a lot here. The Pharisees were accusing Jesus of getting his power from the devil instead of God. They willfully refused to acknowledge the Power of God through Jesus. According to **Mattheew 12: 31** Jesus explained it this way, *"And so I tell you, every kind of sin and slander can be forgiven, but blasphemy against the Spirt will not be forgiven."*

Only those who have turned away from God and His gift of eternal life through Jesus will not be forgiven. Those of us who have ask Jesus to be our savior and have

accepted His gift will be forgiven when we ask. The Pharisees refused to believe that He was the true Messiah, their actions were *deliberate*.

You've heard the story of *the thief on the cross*? Well I recently seen a post on Facebook, and it really made me think about what we as Christians *think* we need to do to be able to get in to heaven when we die. Here's the post, I pray you realize as I did that we don't have to work for our salvation, we cannot earn it .

No baptism, no communion, no confirmation, no speaking in tongues, no mission trip, no volunteering, no financial gifts, and no church clothes. He couldn't even bend his knees to pray. He didn't say the sinner's prayer and among other things, he was a thief. Jesus didn't take way his pain, heal his body, or smite his scoffers. Yet, it was a thief who walked into paradise the same hour as Jesus simply by believing. He had nothing more to offer other than his belief that Jesus was who He said He was. No spin from brilliant theologians. No ego or arrogance. No shiny lights, skinny jeans, or crafty words. No haze machine, donuts, or coffee in the lobby. Just a naked dying man on a cross unable to even fold his hands to pray. (Author unknown)

For God <u>so loved</u> the <u>world</u> that <u>He gave</u> His only Son so that <u>WHOEVER</u> <u>believes</u> in Him <u>will not perish</u> <u>but have everlasting life.</u> John 3:16 NLT <u>Period!!!</u>

He doesn't expect us to jump through hoops to get into heaven, we are not expected to find ways to keep our salvation either. He wants us to have the faith of an innocent child. You know how children believe everything you say to be the truth? How trusting they are? That's the kind of faith we need to have in our relationship with Jesus.

Food for thought

1. Jealousy is toxic, not only for you but for your relationship with others. Share a time in your life that you found yourself jealous of someone, or maybe they were jealous of you. What was the outcome of the situation?

2. What practices and habits can we put into place to help us to fight the temptation to quit?"

3. Describe a time in your childhood that required you to make an adult decision.

4. Describe a time in your life where you've been asked to do something that you felt you were unqualified to do but you couldn't say no. How did it make you feel? What was the outcome of that decision?

5. Are you at a place in your life where you are wrestling with the feeling of being called to do something, but you feel it's too late? Or maybe you're unsure if it's really from God?

Notes

Jealousy is natural but
unnecessary

Chapter 2

Faith verses Fear

When I was a little girl I lived with my aunt, and she was very superstitious. She made me afraid of everything! I know now that she did it out of love. She wanted to keep me safe, and she used my fears to make me obey her, which was a great tool! She made me afraid of the dark. My sister and I used to like to climb into bed with Bidie and sleep with her. She did not like it because we would take up the whole bed she'd say, and it made her hot. and she would tell us after putting us to bed that the boogie man lived under the bed and if we got out in the night he would get us! So went my fear of the dark. Also she'd tell me whenever I climbed up on anything high that I was going to fall and break my neck.

When I was six years old I was at school at recess and playing with a friend who wanted to play on the teeter totter. She sat down on it, and I preceded to climb up to my side, well my friend, as I was climbing and almost to the top my friend began to shake the Teeter Totter, and I fell off on my head and busted my head open . I remember crying and crying. I ended up with twelve stitches. To me that proved what my aunt said was true. So there was the cause of my fear of heights! I thought she was right and whenever I would have to drive over any bridge I became paralyzed to the point I couldn't drive. I avoided bridges and anything that to me would and could hurt me. My point is that fear, that is irrational no matter what they are or how small, can become a crutch and hold us hostage from doing simple things. I have since become braver in my old age and know that the Lord isn't going to let me fall, and if so He'll catch me, and that the boogie man doesn't live under the bed!

Fear though, is a natural part of us. It can keep us from danger. We are built with a natural sense of it, just like all God's creatures, but It can be quite unhealthy too. We can allow our fears to make us afraid of doing anything. Trust me I've been there. We doubt our ability to conquer the most mundane things; like climbing a ladder or going out into the dark by yourself, because you have it in your head that something or someone will harm you. That my friends will hinder us from serving the Lord if we let it.

In the book of Numbers it tells the story of how Moses sent twelve spies to do some research in the land of Canaan. And bring back news to them. Ten came back and gave a pretty grim report of the people and how they compared themselves to the Canaanites and said in **Numbers 13:33** *"we seemed like grasshoppers in our own eyes ."* Some of the people were between seven and nine feet tall. This scared ten of the men. These men, who had witnessed the works of God to this point gave in to their fear and doubted God! They forgot what God had already done for them and didn't think He could protect them and give them the land He had promised! Only two of the twelve who were sent came back with a positive outlook on the situation their names were Caleb and Joshua. They believed God and Caleb even voiced his opinion. He told Moses and Aaron in verse **thirty;** *"We should go up and take possession of the land, for we can certainly do it."* Caleb had faith, real faith as did Joshua. They knew what God could do.

There is a song by *Zac Williams* that is called **"Fear is a Liar"**. The words when I first heard them reminded me of everything I was and still at times are afraid of. He reminds us that *fear* is a spirit from satan and that he will do whatever he can to keep us from living the life that God intended for us. The one verse of the song that struck me goes like this;

Fear, he is a liar

He will take your breath

Stop you in your steps

Fear, he is a liar

He will rob your rest

Steal your happiness

Cast your fear in the fire

Cause fear, he is a liar

That brings me to my next story found in **Joshua chapter 2**. It tells the story of a very brave woman who's lifestyle was less than stellar. She was a Harlot or prostitute if you will, who didn't let her fear stop her from doing what was right. Her name was Rahab. At this particular time the Israelites had been wondering in the desert for forty years. Moses, their leader had died, and God chose Joshua to lead the people. He sent two men into the city of Jericho to spy out the land and bring information back to him They were going to take over the land that God had promised them, and the city of Jerico was one of the places within Cannan. It was a city that was surrounded by high walls that protected the people within against attacks.

Well the home of Rahab was built within the wall itself. I am assuming that men new of her profession and knew to go there for their needs. The two spies must have known this and that is why they chose to go to her home. Again this is my Opinion. I do know that God directs us, the Bible says in **Proverbs 16:9** *"In their hearts Humans plan their course, but the Lord establishes their steps."* God was caring for and protecting the men and he knew the heart of Rahab. You see God went before them; He was caring for them all they had to do was trust. The men could go in undetected, just a couple of customers. They went in and stayed with her **verse 1** says. The king of Jericho was told that the men were Israelites and that they came to spy out the land. The king sent men to Rahab's home and ordered her to bring out the men. But she had hidden them up on the roof. She told the men searching, *"yes the men came to me, but I did not know where they came from. At dusk when it was time to close the city gate, they left. I don't know* *which way they went. Go after them quickly, you may catch up to them." Joshua 2 :4-5.*

She went up to the roof and told the two men that the people of her land heard about all the miracles their God was doing for them and *that a great fear had fallen on them.* she tells them in **verse 11:** ***"when we heard of it our hearts melted and everyone's courage failed because of you, <u>for the Lord your God is God in heaven above and on the earth below.</u>"*** You see, in the story of Rahab it tells that they all knew who the God of the Israelites was and what He could do, but only Rahab chose to believe and follow Him. She goes on to beg them to protect her and her family from being destroyed. The men made a deal with her and told her to place a scarlet cord in the window and she would be protected along with everyone in her household. But if anyone came out of the home they would be destroyed. Does that remind you of another story? I love how the whole Bible seems to conjoin within each story.

For example, in **Joshua 2:17-19**, the spies tell Rahab to place a *red cord* in the window for which she let them down, and that would tell them not to destroy her home. Likewise, in the book of **Exodus 12** it tells the story of the Israelites and how they were to put *blood* on the door posts of their home to protect them from when the Lord went through and killed every first-born Egyptian male child. He told Moses that He would pass over those homes, and they would be protected as long as they remained indoors.

There was so much fear, anxiety and doubts that Rahab could have yielded to, but she had a decision to make. She was a working woman trying to provide for her family. She minded her own business. And then an upheaval came into her life in the form of two men. I mean, why did she feel she had to hide them? Well, I believe that God knew her heart was open to Him. And that she, when hearing all the stories of what their God was doing for them, maybe, just maybe she decided to *trust*. She did what was asked of her.

The King sent men to Rahab's home to tell her to bring them out. But she lied! She told the king's men that they were there, but they had left, And all the while they were hiding up on her roof. She was very resourceful, hiding them the way she did. Rahab didn't allow her fears to keep her from being used by God. She acted because of her faith, and God rewarded her for it!

We need to remember that Jericho was a pagan city *"believing in anything but the God of creation,"* that God was giving to the Israelites. But Rahab's faith allowed her act, and she remained obedient, even at a great cost to her. She was risking her life. Rahab didn't let mistakes, and her past keep her from serving the Lord, and neither should we. God doesn't look at our history, **Isaiah 43:25** reminds us of God's faithfulness. ***"I even I am He who blots out your transgressions, for my own sake, and remembers your sins no more."*** He doesn't have a naughty or nice list like Santa. People who know who God is but choose to go their own way and give in to their selfish desires will miss out on so much.

When we look at the word "Fear" it almost always evokes a feeling of dread. Because we naturally assume that to "fear" someone or something we are to be afraid. The dictionary puts it this way. *an unpleasant often strong emotion caused by anticipation or awareness of danger. [Merriam Webster].* But when we see the word in the Bible we need to look at the context for which it was written.

So when Rahab spoke of being in great fear she was speaking of being afraid of what she knew their God would do to her and her people. She had heard the stories and knew their God protected them. So she was willing to do what the men wanted her to do because She had hope that the God of the Israelites would save her if she was obedient to Him. In spite of her fears she became bold.

In the New Testament Jesus was always telling his disciples to not be afraid, but to try and overcome their fear with believing in and trusting in Him. Now fear and worry are closely related in terms of our anxiety. For example; to *fear* something means that we can see what is causing us to be anxious, whereas *worry* is often thinking about something we feel or imagine could happen but isn't present at the moment.

For example, I am getting ready to fly across the country to vacation with family and I "hate" to fly! It is the one thing that I am most fearful of. I get nauseous thinking about it. when the time comes to actually board the plane, I'm shaking and sweating. Not a good thing for someone who claims to love and trust the Lord, right? I will sit there in my seat, and when we begin to taxi down the runway, I sit up and try to bend forward and hang on, so I don't fall out of the back of the plane!   That is how my mind works. My family laughs and thinks it's funny. But God doesn't. He is there and when I focus on Him, He provides for me every time! Someone will always be there to distract me. Or my favorite is when the pilot takes off, it's a grádual ascent not straight up. The funny thing is whenever I try and get something, like a pill or yes, alcohol to help with my fears I am never able to get it. God says no, Cathy, you're going to have to trust me! So this time I'm going to trust Him and know that He is with me and like a friend said one time, "If your meant to die in an airplane nothing will stop you from doing so!" Not so comforting, but still she's not wrong.

Now in **Psalm 103** when David speaks of fear, he is speaking in terms of reverence, awe, or respect for God as well as love. In **verses 12-13** David explains God's mercy and love for those who are his children.

"as far as the east is from the west, so far has He removed our transgressions from us. As a father has compassion on his children, the Lord has compassion on those who fear Him."

To make a long story even longer,: Rahab went on to live with the Israelites and married a Israelite named Salmon and became an ancestor of David and of Jesus! See**, {Matthew 1:5; Hebrews 11:31}** God can and will use anyone. We don't need a degree or have wealth to be used by God we just need to be willing.

Just as I know that God wants me to write and tell my story through these Bible studies, even though I don't feel qualified to do so. God chose me and after playing tug of war with Him, I said ok, I'll give it a shot. I had to step out on faith and know that **fear is a liar!**

One of my favorite Christian artists is Lauren Daigle. When I listen to Christian music I know God has brought me a special message. One of her songs is *"Hold on to me."* *The verse that really resonates with me personally is:* ***When I'm not somebody that I believe in, Hold on to me. When I miss the light the night has stolen and I'm slammin' all the doors you've open, hold on to me"***.

I cannot tell you all the opportunities I've missed out on because of the fear and doubt of not being good enough or smart enough. I keep hearing all the negative comments made about me as a child in a dysfunctional household that even as fifty plus years has passed, I keep hearing and sometimes believing. I get sucked in, into a vortex of self- hatred that God does not like, and He is always there reminding me that I am good enough, that I am precious in His eyes. Whether through his word, music or through people that He has brought into my life. So remember the next time a negative thought comes to mind, that you are a Child of the most High and He loved you enough that He sent His only son to die for you!

In the New testament, in the book of **Hebrews chapter eleven,** it is known as the *"Hall of Faith"* chapter. Now these people not only believed but acted on those beliefs. Rahab being one of them. It says in verse thirty-one: *"By faith the prostitute Rahab, because she welcomed the spies, was not killed with those who were disobedient."*

Hebrews 11:1 says, *"Now faith is <u>confidence</u> in what we hope for and <u>assurance</u> about what we do not see."*

Hebrews 12:1-2 says, *" Therefore since we are surrounded by such a great cloud of witnesses, let us throw off everything that hinders and the sin that so easily entangles. And let us run with perseverance the race marked out for us, fixing our eyes on Jesus, the pioneer and perfecter of faith."*

I love the part where it says *"let us run with perseverance the race marked out for us"* Paul is essentially saying that we as *Christ followers* are to *keep going and not quit. God has a plan for each of us* and though it may be hard and frustrating, as long as *we keep our focus on Jesus* we will win the Race.

The Bible says that if we have the faith of a mustard seed, we can move mountains.

Jesus was trying to explain to his disciples the reason they could not drive out the demon from the man in question. Jesus said it was, **Matthew 17:20**, *"Because you have so little faith. Truly I tell you, if you have faith as small as a mustard seed you can say to this mountain, Move from here to there, and it will move. Nothing will be impossible for you."*

He is asking of us the same. If we have faith, then we will be able to remove anything that stands in our way. Ask yourself, what is standing in your way and keeping you from having mountain moving faith? Is it *unbelief?* Are you *faithless?* Is it *fear* that people will find you odd? What are the obstacles Aka *"Mountains"* that is keeping you from walking with Jesus and truly allowing Him to work in your life?

Me? I tend to want to be in control all the time. And when I feel I am losing that control, I freak out. Jesus hasn't given up on me though. He is walking with me and keeping me on the path. The Bible says not to fear the ones who can kill the body but fear the one whom can kill the body and soul. **Matthew 10:28.**

Did you know that In the Bible the word **fear** is mentioned over *one hundred and thirty times*! That should tell us something right? God is telling us to fear Him not the world.

Jesus was preparing His disciples for persecution that would come because of their faith in Him. He told them; *I am sending you out like sheep among the wolves. Therefore be as shrewd as snakes and as innocent as doves. Matthew 10:16(NIV).* There's a lot going on in that verse let's look at the examples Jesus gives.

A <u>snake</u> is always on the lookout for predators and food in order to survive. The snake is very still and is always watching out for themselves. They are always on guard. **Genesis 3:1** says that the serpent *AKA snake* was crafty and subtle. He snuck up on Eve in the garden and before she knew what was happening he convinced her that everything she believed about God was questionable. It can happen to us today if we're not careful. We, not unlike Eve, need to be on guard against those who, like the devil wants to keep us from walking with the Lord. The devil will bring people into your life that will tempt you and try and convince you like he did Eve. "Don't be an EVE!"

Doves were considered clean; harmless. They were used as sacrifices. We too are called to be wise and yet innocent. We must know who our audience is. We are called to be gentle but not pushovers. Or as my aunt always told me, *"Don't be a rug!, don't let people walk all over you!"*

1Peter 2:12 says, in the midst of suffering we are to *"Live such good lives among the pagans that, though they accuse you of doing wrong, they may see your good deeds and glorify God on the day He visits us."*

The world is the same today as it was during Jesus' time on earth. Hostile toward followers of Jesus. Jesus was sending his disciples out and warning them that they were going as sheep among wolves. *Wolves* are predators and they are always hunting for food; they will always look for the weakest and easiest prey so that they will have the upper hand and get their meal. while *sheep* are innocent, and they depend on someone to look out for them and keep them safe. They live in flocks, if one wanders from the flock then it becomes easy prey for the wolves.

Like sheep we too must stick together and help one another on this journey of the Christian faith. We will learn from one another and have the skills to reach others for Christ.

Food for Thought

1. Martin Luther King Jr. said it best; *"Faith is taking the first step even when you don't see the whole staircase."*

   Describe what you see as the biggest obstacle that may be keeping you from stepping out in faith?

2. Share a time when you felt the Lord asking you to step out on faith. How did you respond?

   As a child I was often ridiculed by the adults in my life, and I carried that stigma into my adulthood. It took me many, many years, along with the Lord's love for me to overcome it.

   One of my favorite verses in the Bible is, **Jeremiah 29:11, "For I know the plans I have for you", declares the Lord, "plans to prosper you and not to harm you, plans to give you hope and a future."**

3. Is there something or someone in your life that is keeping you from acting on God's desire for you? If so, what steps do you need to take to be rid of the negativity that is keeping you from serving Christ?

4. Remember the Spirit of God lives inside us and will give us the strength to do what He wants us to do. What can you do today to begin your journey of being a leader for Christ?

5. Recall a time in your life when you prayed a prayer of desperation thinking that God will answer right away, only to still be waiting. Do you feel that at times The Lord seems aloof to your needs? If so what can you do to change your *stink'n think'n?*

Notes

Faith in God changes
everything!

Chapter 3

What I think ~ verses ~ what God Knows

Mother Teresa comes to mind when I think of being a woman who is called into leadership for the Lord. She has a great and awe-inspiring story. In her diary she wrote of all the things she went through, and how God Got her through it.

Mother Teresa felt that she heard the call of her inner conscience to serve the poor of India for Jesus.

Teresa experienced what she later described as *"the call within the call"*. She says, *"I was to leave the convent and help the poor while living among them. It was an order. To fail would have been to break the faith."*

Mother Teresa wrote in her diary that her first year was *"fraught with difficulty."* With no income, she begged for food and supplies and experienced doubt, loneliness, and the temptation to return to the comfort of convent life during those early months. She goes on to say,

"Our Lord wants me to be a free nun covered with the poverty of the cross. Today, I learned a good lesson. The poverty of the poor must be so hard for them. While looking for a home I walked and walked till my arms and legs ached. I thought how much they must ache in body and soul, looking for a home, food, and health. Then, the comfort of Loreto (her former congregation) *came to tempt me. "You have only to say the word and all that will be yours again", the Tempter kept on saying. ... Of free choice, my God, and out of love for you, I desire to remain and do whatever be your Holy will in my regard. I did not let a single tear come."*

Mother Teresa had many health issues which included two heart attacks, malaria, and a broken collarbone that caused her to be hospitalized. She went hungry. She said that *"the hunger for love is much more difficult to remove than the hunger for bread."*

She led a life of conviction, purpose, and compassion. But more than anything she led a life of faith. She said of those she served, *"each one of them is Jesus in disguise."*

God used her because she was willing to listen and accept the call God had for her.

I mean don't get me wrong, we cannot all be like Mother Teresa, but we can all have a *willing heart* when we hear the call by God. She went on to say that *"Your true character Is most accurately measured by how you treat those who can do 'Nothing' for you."* That my friends is the most inspiring statement I have ever heard and will try to always remember them as I come in contact with others.

I can relate to what Mother Teresa said about being *"called within the call."* She was called to be a Nun, then God decided to call her to do more. I too had such a calling, but unlike Mother Teresa, I said nope, not going to do that!

As a young Christian I knew I was to teach children the Bible. It came easy for me. I was able to memorize scripture and show the children how to do it as well. I also was able to show them how to apply it to their daily lives. I did that for nearly thirty years. Then it the midst of teaching the little ones, I felt the need to teach women how to read and study scripture. It was a call from the Lord that I tried to ignore, but in the end began to do so. Believe me God is relentless when wanting us to do His will.

Years ago I belonged to a small group of women that was having a hard time getting past their past, I being one of them. when one day I felt the Lord pushing me to help these women, but more importantly, to help them understand Scripture and how God can get us through the hard stuff. I was co-leading with a friend a study in which it required a lot of reading. When asked, no one seemed to be willing to read so my friend and I did most of the reading. One evening as we were in the group reading, my friend asked if someone would be willing to read, to which one woman spoke up and said, *"Cathy seems to know all about the Bible let her do it."* For the life of me I could not understand why she didn't like me! I quit leading after that. I was afraid I guess of what others would think of me, like the woman in the group. My point is that there are haters out there that Satan uses to stop you in your tracks. He did me. But God is bigger than that, He never gave up on me. He is willing to use us in spite of us. We cannot allow negative people to stop us from serving the Lord.

I was told years later that Satan knew we were making great strides with women new to the faith, and he would do whatever he could to stop it. He temporarily succeeded! For nearly fifteen years I wouldn't even consider teaching ladies. I felt I wasn't good enough, smart enough, you name it. I decided God needed someone a lot smarter than me.

When my husband and I moved to Florida and found a church, I met a few women that God kept putting in my face. I have a saying; ***"Lord why have you put this person in my face? And what do you want me to do with them?"*** One evening after Bible study a woman came up to me and ask me if I'd be willing to teach her one on one how to understand what we were studying and how to look up scripture. She told me she felt so lost in class that she was getting ready to quit. So began my journey of teaching ladies how to study the Bible.

I came up with a curriculum that was simple to use and very basic so the women could understand how to venture into the Word. I called it Bible 101. When we were done with the Bible study, I was asked when Bible 102 was coming out. That is when I began my journey in writing books and telling my story of how God never let go of me and used me in spite of my fears.

I was encouraged to continue to write and teach. God is so patient with us. Just as He was with so many people in Scripture, He will be patient with us a well.

God uses common Ordinary people just like you and me to accomplish His will.

When we resist the call God has for us, it is usually because all we see is our limitations and weaknesses, or like my aunt used to tell me, I couldn't *see the forest for the trees.* We fail to see the gift He has given us, because all we are willing to see is what is in front of us. We have blinders on. We need to learn to take them off so we can see the whole picture.

Remember Jonah ran away from what God wanted him to do. But the Lord never gave up on him. Moses; Gideon; Elijah and Sarah to name a few all-doubted God's plan for them and His word and questioned Him. But in spite of their worries and doubts God used them successfully.

I used to be a Transportation Bus assistant. My job was to keep the kids behaving while the Driver drove them to and from School. There are cameras as well as audio on every bus, and it's always being recorded, for our protection as well as the Children.

Children can be very hateful and mean when they want to be. But my Job was to smile and either down play the incident or to ignore it completely. If the situation became too much then I would need to report the incident to the school by way of an incident report and a referral for the child.

Like I said I was there to assist the driver. I would report any serious incident to them and then hopefully together we can work the situation out before it gets to the point of writing up or getting a child kicked off the bus.

My point to all this is, the cameras remind me that someone is always watching me and my back. God is watching our backs and guiding us to behave and help others and not be critical. Remember we cannot control others behavior, but we can control how we react to them. I know that I have been called to serve the Lord in this capacity, as well as to be a light to those around me.

Like I've said before, I'm a morning person and basically a happy person. I smile and hope that when I do, I give that person whom I shared that smile with a little bit of hope for the day. Make their day a little brighter. And I pray for them. I have no idea what is going on in that person's life and why they act the way they do.

My job as a follower of Christ is not to judge them but love them and show them Jesus. We may never go on a mission in another country or feed thousands of people, but you and I can reach one person at a time. You never know who you will run into that needs that smile or that good morning.

While you're standing in line at the grocery store, or maybe you're in line at the drive thru, just look around at all the people and just start praying for them or if you are able pay for the grumpy gentleman's groceries who is impatiently standing behind you thinking you're taking way too long, and he only has a few items. *Small steps is all that is required.* In **Matthew 22:39** it says, *"you shall love your neighbor as yourself."*

Within the Church we are known as the *"body"* of Christ. Like the human body that has many parts to keep us alive and going, so does the body of the church. Paul explained this to the church in Corinth. In **1 Corinthians chapter 12** Paul was explaining the different gifts within the body and how we are to use them for the good and the growth within the church.

Paul told them that there are different types of gifts, but they are all from the Holy Spirit, and there are different types of service, but we serve the same Lord. In **verse 7** Paul puts it this way; *"A spiritual gift is given to each of us so we can help each other."* (NLT) not one gift or person within the church is better or greater than the other. We are all called to the same purpose, *"To serve Christ, and build His church"*

I know that each one us has our own personality, and I also know that we need to look beyond one another's faults or the one person who is an *EGR* or *extra grace required.* what we perceive as a fault may just be that they are going through something we know nothing about. we need to get along and know that what we are doing is building the church for Jesus. *It's not about us;* it's always about Him.

Paul explains that the roles of each person may be different than another person, but with the same goal. He goes on to say that some may be called to give wise advice, some are good at having great faith. Which brings me to a memory of when I first became a follower of Jesus.

I remember when I was attending a church and became friends with a woman whom I thought had it all together and I admired that, because I just knew that I was a hot mess and could maybe learn something. She was a very calm person and soft-spoken. Whenever she would pray she was so eloquent and when she spoke she was so calm and seemed like she knew just what to say. Nothing seemed to bother her. I thought, I want to be like that. Calm and hopeful to where nothing bothered me, and I wanted to trust the Lord completely like my friend seemed to do. I didn't know it then, but now I know that God had given her the gift of faith. He gives all kinds of gifts and not everyone gets the same. Now I'm not saying that just because some of us doesn't have that particular gift it does not mean that we're faithless, it just means that it comes easier for some than it does for others. Some of us has to work at it a little harder that's all. We have to make a conscience decision to trust and believe that God will answer, and His answer will be for the best.

In an article by **"Got Questions.Org"** they explain it this way regarding one who has the gift of faith. *As with all spiritual gifts, the gift of faith is given to some Christians who then use it to edify others in the body of Christ. Those with the gift of faith are an inspiration to their fellow believers, exhibiting a simple confidence in God that shows in all they say and do.* That was my friend. It goes on to say that, *Extraordinarily faithful people show a humble godliness and reliance on God's promises, often so much so that they are known to be quietly fearless and zealous. They are so convinced that all obstacles to the gospel and to God's purposes will be overcome and so confident that God will secure the advancement of His cause, that they will often do far more in the promotion of His kingdom than the most talented and erudite preachers and teachers.* That, ladies and gentlemen was my friend.

Paul instructed the Corinthians to examine themselves, to look inside and test themselves to see if their faith was real or not. I challenge you to sit back and really examine your life as a follower of Jesus, then you can truly see what His plan is for you, if you choose the path of following the Lord.

Then when you are done you can figure out what your specific gifts are. Ask the Lord to show you so you can begin to use yours for the good of the body, as well as to reach non-believers. Every one of us is called to reach others for Jesus. **1 John 3:18** puts it this way, *"Little children, let us not love in word or talk, but is deed and in truth". (NKJV)* this way when people look at you and see the real you they will know that you are a follower of Jesus, and it will show that you are genuine in your faith.

My gift is the gift of *Hospitality*, which I didn't understand at the time, but now I do. I know that it just comes naturally to me. I love to entertain, and I love to help others. I am always willing to help another person who is in need. I never knew that it was a gift from the Lord, but it is.

I imagine that Peter's wife and mother-in-law were very good at it. I mean Peter's mother-in-law was very sick and in **Luke chapter 4 verses 38-39** tells the story of how Jesus went to visit them and found the woman in bed with a high fever, and they had asked Jesus to help her. **Verse 39** says, *So he bent over her and rebuked the fever, and it left her. She got up at once and began to wait on them.*

Wow that tells us that He healed her to the point that all her weakness from the sickness left, she was feeling great! She was strong enough to get up and wait on the guests. I mean, I would think I'd need a shower first or something, right? She was whole and complete, and she used her gift of hospitality to serve Jesus and the disciples. We don't know her name; all we know is who she was related to and her health issues. But the very important message that I got out of the short story was that she used her gift that God gave her willingly. We too should look inside of ourselves and find the gift that the Holy Spirit has given us and use it for the good of the Kingdom.

Prayer is another gift, that even though everyone and anyone can and should talk to the Lord, it is still a gift to some people. I've met some prayer warriors over the years, and I am so impressed how they come up with the most eloquent words to use to speak to the Lord, Me? Nope. That is not something I'm gifted with. I mean I talk to the Lord all the time and He knows what I'm saying, and He gets me, He knows that I am sincere when speaking with Him. That is all that is required. People will come up to me and they know that I am a Christian, and they'll tell me to pray for and them, or they'll tell me their issues, and I will be brave enough at times to stop right where we are and pray with them, even though I feel I am awkward at praying. Jesus doesn't care. And neither do the ones I'm standing in prayer with.

Jesus often went away to pray by himself. In **Luke 4:42** (CEV) it says that ***Jesus went out to a place where He could be alone,*** but people were always looking for him. He rarely was alone. even Jesus needed time by himself, maybe to pray or maybe to just try and collect himself. We all need that as well. Jesus was completely God, but He was completely human as well and He had needs just like us. He was tired and exhausted I'd imagine from healing and dealing with people. If Jesus needed alone time how much more do we need to be alone with God and take time to pray.

I know from experience that sometimes we try and do too much when it comes to serving, that too can become a hindrance or a stumbling block in our walk to where we want to quit serving. Jesus knew His limitations as a human and knew when He needed to be alone to pray or like I said to collect His thoughts.

In **Matthew chapter six**, Jesus is teaching about prayer. Jesus tells the people in **verse 5** that when you pray you are not supposed to act like the religious leaders. They prayed out in the open where they could be seen and heard, they wanted attention from others. They weren't doing it for God; they were doing it for themselves. Jesus called them Hypocrites. The word **Hypocrite** according to the dictionary is *a person who puts on a false appearance of virtue or religion.* In the Greek *(hypokrites)* it means *"answerer, actor on a stage, pretender."* In essence it is someone who wears a mask of being moral when their actions show their true colors. Jesus told the disciples to not be that way, he said in verse six; *"But when you pray, go into your room, close the door, and pray to the Father, who is unseen. Then your Father, who sees what is done in secret, will reward you."*

Praying fancy words or praying for a long time in front of others isn't what is required, it doesn't impress the Lord, just be yourself and pray from the heart.

So you see not everyone has the gift of, let's say, "speech", because in reality that is what it is. Have you ever been in a prayer group or with someone who just seems to know the right words to say? I have and it's a beautiful thing to listen to. Am I envious? Yes, at times. I feel so inadequate when my turn to pray comes around, especially if I'm next to the one who was so great at it. But like I said I've learned that The Lord doesn't want nor expect perfection, He just wants my sincerity of heart. I should not worry about what others think of me and what I feel are my awkward prayers.

I have to ask myself who am I trying to please? The group I'm with or God? Romans 8:26-27 says *In the same way, the Spirit helps us in our weakness. We do not know what we ought to pray for, but the spirit Himself intercedes for us with groans the words cannot express, And He who searches our hearts knows the mind of the Spirit, because the Spirit intercedes for the saints in accordance with God's will.*

That my friends is awesome! Knowing that we are not alone. we have someone who is always there with us and will help us with our prayers to the Lord and will help us when we feel we are not good enough to do anything. All we have to do is ask.

Food for thought

God will place people in our path for many reasons. Sometimes it's so we can be helpful to that person, or sometimes it's so they can be a comfort for us. Regardless of the situation, it's an opportunity for growth in our relationship with Jesus, whom will never leave us alone.

1. Describe a time when God placed someone in your life that treated you unfairly. What was the outcome?

2. While serving the Lord, was there ever a time you wanted to quit? Why or why not?

3. Sometimes we think we know what God wants from us. We decide to serve Him where we feel the most comfortable. Is God nudging you to serve Him in a different aspect? Are you listening, or resisting? Why?

4. Were there ever a time in your life that you felt the need to pray for some stranger in a public setting? How did that make you feel? What did you do about it?

The book of James talks a lot about trials and temptations. In **James 1:2** he says to *"consider it pure joy my brothers and sisters whenever you face trials of many kinds. Because you know that the testing of your faith produces perseverance."*

5. Describe at least two good things that have come from the trials in your life?

Notes

"Once you learn to quit, it
becomes a habit"

Vince Lombardi

Chapter 4

Drama, Drama, Drama!

The Bible is made up of sixty-six books. The Old Testament and the New testament. Now if you have read any of the 39 that are in the Old Testament you would know that there is nothing but drama! That's where my next lady comes in at. she is found in the book that is named after her. *Esther.*

Now Esther, before she became "Esther", was named Hadassah. She was a young Hebrew, a virgin and beautiful to look at. She was raised by her older cousin Mordecai because her parents had died. They lived in the capital city of Susa, in the province of Persia.

Hopefully you get the picture. Meanwhile back at the Palace... there was a king named Xerxes, and this man loved to party! He was the king of the province where Mordecai and Esther lived. This was not a Hebrew friendly place.

The king after many days of drinking and partying, decided that he would send for the Queen, her name was Vashti. Now Queen Vashti refused the kings request!

This was unheard of! From what I've learned King Xerxes had a temper and drank like a fish; this my friends is not a good combination. This I assumed made everyone walk on eggshells around him, especially when he was drinking.

When the queen refused to come as ordered, This made the king extremely upset so much so that he asked his advisors what he should do with her To save face. They told him that he had to show other wives of not only his, but his nobles as well that they were not to defy their husbands, so he made it a law. In **Esther 1:16-21** tells the story of what his advisors said. Basically to put her away and she was never to enter the presence of the king again, and to send a message to everyone that the women should behave and listen to their husbands. Drama!

Respect is a two-way street. I mean the women may have obeyed fearing the consequences, but trust me when I say, they did not respect their husbands for treating them like possessions. King Xerxes liked to collect things, and beautiful women were one of them. remember the harem? Yea that's a lot of women!

King Xerxes sent a decree to all of the provinces of his kingdom and commanded that all the beautiful and young virgin women be brought to his home so he could choose a new queen.

Esther was among those chosen. She was afraid I could imagine. She was ordered by her cousin Mordecai not to reveal her nationality because people hated the

Hebrew people. In **verses 10-11 of Esther** it says: *Esther had not revealed her nationality and family background, because Mordecai had forbidden her to do so. Every day he walked back and forth near the courtyard of the harem to find out how Esther was and what was happening to her.*

He was worried about her. She stayed in the harem for a year getting ready for her turn to come before the king. She made such a good impression on him that out of all the women, the king chose Esther.

There is a song by *Katie Nichole and Big Daddy Weave* called " ***God is in this Story.***" It is one that reminds me that I'm never alone and that the Lord is always there, and I can count on him to get me through anything! My favorite part of the song is;

God is in this story

God is in the details

Even in the broken parts

He holds my heart, He never fails

When I'm at my weakest

I will trust in Jesus

Always in the highs and lows

The One who goes before me

God is in this story.

I can imagine that was the way Esther felt. She was trusting God to get her through a very tough time in her young life.

Later when after Esther becomes queen and her uncle Mordecai, while sitting at the kings gate overhears a conspiracy to kill the king, he tells Esther who in turn went to tell the king what her cousin overheard and gave him the credit. So a long story made even longer, a noble by the name of Haman who was appointed second in command to the King, People were to bow down to this guy. When Haman found out that Mordecai would not do so he became enraged, he decided that Mordecai had to die. Not just Mordecai but all the Jews. He hated the fact that the Jewish people would refused to bow down to him. He hated what Mordecai stood for. *God as the only one to be bowed to,* so when Mordecai found out he put on sackcloth and ashes.

This is the way the Jewish people would mourn. It showed that they were in great distress. **Verse 4 of chapter 4** says that when the queen heard of this she became in great distress and wanted him to put clothes on. She had no idea what the problem with Mordecai was. But Mordecai refused and told her why and insisted that the queen do something to stop it She told Mordecai that the rules of going before the king without permission could result in her death! **Esther 4:12-14** says: When Esther's words were reported to Mordecai, he sent back this answer: *"do not think that because you are in the Kings house you alone of all the Jews will escape. For if you remain silent at this time, relief*

and deliverance will arise from another place, but
you and your father's family will perish. But who
knows that you have come to your royal position for
such a time as this?"

I just love that verse! Mordecai was reminding Esther that God is in control and if she wasn't willing to do what he felt she was called to do, God would send someone else. Like I have stated before, God's will, will be done with me or without me. But to miss out on such a blessing is so sad. Yes she was scared! I mean I would be too! But that is where our faith must take center stage. When we are hanging by a thread dangling over a cliff with no one there but God. That's when we find him if we have faith. We must come to him with a sincere heart, knowing he will answer us. Even though we don't have a clue of the outcome. We must trust God knows what He is doing, and know it is for our good.

Esther had all her household fast and pray before she went to the king even though she was not summoned to do so. She went and the king was pleased to see her and allowed her to come before his throne. She then requested that he and Haman come and dine at the banquet she had prepared for them. so they went and the king was willing to give her half of his kingdom he told her. But she said come again tomorrow evening and I will tell you then. So they showed up again the next night and after a leisurely dinner she was again asked what he could do for her. Now this whole time Haman was thinking that he was being honored and bragged about it to his wife and friends the night before, and they even suggested that he set up a pole in the kings court and have Mordecai impaled on it! WOW. I told you, Drama!

Esther 7:3-4 says: *"If I have found favor with you, your Majesty, and if it pleases you, grant me my life- this is my petition. and spare my people- this is my request. For I and my people have been sold to be destroyed, killed, and annihilated. If we were merely sold as male and female slaves, I would have kept quiet, because no such distress would justify disturbing the King."*

This upset the King greatly and he wanted to know who would dare do such a thing. Esther says in **verse 6**, *An adversary and enemy! This vile Haman!*

Well, you know that pole Haman had set up? Well the king ordered that he be impaled on his own contraption. They then reversed the decree to which all the Jews were to be killed, and the Jews were delivered.

Please Read the Book of Esther, it is so fascinating! God is not mentioned in the book, but you can see on every page where He was and how He was working for the good of the Jews. She had a choice to make and chose to do the right thing even at a cost.

We too have a choice to make. Are we going to set back and hope someone else will do it, or will we choose to be brave enough to do it ourselves? Trust me when I say I have set back and watched as the world went by and even knowing I was missing out on so many blessings the Lord had for me. I didn't budge, until a woman desperate to know God's word showed me that I had no choice but to help. I always prayed to the Lord and asked what my purpose was, why He would not show me. But He did, several times and I just ignored it.

I sometimes wondered if I was being foolish in thinking I could do something that I thought was way beyond my capabilities, but I would've been wrong! The Holy Spirit was showing me and answering my prayer. It's like the Holy Spirit was calling me and I'd pick up only to think it was the wrong number. I kept hanging up! He made a way for me to be able to do His will. I know one thing is true, and that is we need to recognize when the Holy Spirit is calling us, and when we choose to answer He will make it possible for us to do His will. He gives us the right tools to do whatever He has asked of us. Proverbs 3:5-6 says; ***Trust in the Lord with all your heart and lean not on your own understanding; in all your ways acknowledge Him and He will direct your path.*** (NKJV)

That is one of my favorite verses I say to myself. Whenever I get into my head and start to doubt my abilities and what the Lord has asked of me, which is the devil whispering in my ear, by the way. The Holy spirit brings this verse to my thoughts and then I remember who God is and what I am to Him. Let's break this verse down and find out the context of it.

To trust is a huge thing in of itself. _Trust_ in the Websters puts this way; ***Belief in the honesty and reliability of another.*** _Lean_ ***means bend or slant; to*** *rely on something; rest against something.* <u>*Acknowledge*</u> *means to admit or recognize; to respond to; Express thanks.* That verse tells me that I am to believe what Jesus says and to rest on Him and to give Him thanks for He is the one that is on my side.

One of My favorite stories in the Bible is in **John chapter 13,** and in **verse 23** in the NKJV it says: *Now there was laying on Jesus' bosom one of His disciples, whom Jesus loved.* That was the cultural way of eating at banquets by the way. So picture everyone lying on the floor with a low table and food on it. They weren't in chairs like we do.

John recognized Jesus' love for him, and he leaned on him, he trusted Him. Jesus is asking that of us today. I know that I would love to be able to lean back on Jesus when I see Him face to face. But until then, I am learning to lean on His promises and know that He's looking out for my well-being and yours too.

We need to trust in His word to help us serve Him and know that we can trust Him to care for us. We also need to acknowledge that fact and respond accordingly.

Isaiah 6:8 says: *Then I heard "the voice" of the Lord saying, Whom shall I send? And who will go for us? And I said, "here I am, Send me!"*

That is what I want to be able to say, *"Send me!"* I want that for you as well! We cannot do anything in our own power, but with the Lord guiding us, we can do the impossible.

One of my favorite Hymns in church that we sang every week is called "Leaning on the Everlasting Arms"

[Verse 1]

What a fellowship, what a joy divine

Leaning on the everlasting arms;

What a blessedness, what a peace is mine

Leaning on the everlasting arms

[Chorus]

Leaning, leaning

Safe and secure from all alarm

Leaning, leaning

Leaning on the everlasting arms

[Verse 2]

O how sweet to walk in this pilgrim way

Leaning on the everlasting arms;

O how bright the path grows from day to day

Leaning on the everlasting arms

[Chorus]

Leaning, leaning

Safe and secure from all alarm

Leaning, leaning

Just leaning on the everlasting arms

This hymn comes from a gentleman named Anthony Showalter. He was a musician who wrote it along with his friend Elisha Hoffman in 1887 whom After hearing of two of his students losing their wives and were buried the same day. This was I imagine was a terrible time for the men and such an encouragement for them at the same time.

It is based on the Scripture **Deuteronomy 33:27.** *The eternal God is your refuge, and underneath are the everlasting arms, He will thrust out the enemy before you and will say "Destroy!"*

We too can experience the peace that comes from learning to lean on and trust God and His desire for our lives.

Food for thought

1. Think back on a time when you were asked to do something that was out of your comfort zone. How did you respond?

2. Trying new things can be terrifying, but it can also cause you to grow into a stronger person of faith. Contemplate on what would be the best/worst case scenario. What does that look like? Now ask yourself *"Am I going to let fear of the unknown paralyze me?"* Am I looking to the Lord for help?

3. Fear is a biggie for me, and satan knows this. So when I am afraid to move in the direction the Lord is taking me, I am learning to take the time to pray and read the Bible and He shows me exactly what He wants and comforts me. I then realize that Jesus is there holding out His hand for me to grab onto. What fear is holding you back from serving?

4. When God called me out to write Bible studies, I felt that surely I was mistaken and getting in over my head. But the Lord continue to be patient with me, nudging me along a path that I didn't fell qualified for at all!

    Is God calling you to do something for him, right now? If so, explain.

5. My favorite verse in the Bible is **Jeremiah 29:11, *"for I know the plans I have for you, declares the Lord, plans to prosper you not to harm you, plans to give you hope and a future."***

    Do you believe that the Lord is for you and not against you? Can you look back and see where the Lord has been coaxing you along?

Notes

Life begins at the end of your comfort zone

Neale Donald Walsch

Chapter 5

Family Ties

This is a story of determination and faithfulness. This next chapter is about two women who have only two things in common and that is faith in God and loss of a loved one. I'm speaking about Naomi and Ruth. Their story is found in the book of **Ruth**, named after the woman who was determined to stay and help her mother-in-law Naomi. Naomi was from Bethlehem. When a famine hit the area of their hometown she and her family moved to the land of Moab. There in Moab the people were hostile toward the Israelites. Here was where her two sons met, and married women named Orpah and Ruth. Naomi's husband and both sons died, and left Naomi decimated, I can only imagine, I mean I know I would be. When time came for Naomi to return to her homeland of Bethlehem, she told her daughters-in-law goodbye and for them to return to their families and *their gods*. Orpah did so but Ruth refused, she told Naomi in **chapter 1: 16-17,** ***"Don't urge me to leave you or to turn back from you. Where you go I will go, and where you stay I will stay. Your people will be my people and your God My God. Where you die , I will die, and there I will be***

buried. May the Lord deal with me, be it ever so severely, if even death separates you and me."

I love how passionate Ruth is when it comes to wanting to stay with her Mother-in-law. Ruth and Orpah had witnessed for almost ten years the faith of Naomi, her faithfulness during such a trying time in her life, of losing first her husband then both her sons! And what a great witness she was to her sons wives. She showed them her faith in God when everyone around her was living to please themselves, she chose to trust in the one that she knew could get her through tough times.

Naomi and her family lived during the time of when the Israelites lived as they wanted. Joshua who had lead the people and guided them the right way died. The Israelites became lazy and selfish and disobeyed the commands of God. **Judges 17:6** says: *In those days Israel had no king; everyone did as they saw fit.* That was the reason for the famine. They were being punished for their disobedience. But Naomi remained faithful. The land of Moab had plenty of food so she and her husband and two sons moved there, even though they knew that the people would be against them. Naomi trusted God to care for them.

Ruth was the wife of Naomi's son Mahlon. After ten years the Bible says that both of Naomi's sons passed away and so now we have three widows. Naomi, Orpah, and Ruth. when Naomi heard that the famine in her homeland was over with, she decided to return to what she knew. Her daughter -in-laws wanted to go with her and said as much. But Naomi urged them to go back to their families so they could provide for them. Naomi was a widow and could not provide for them financially or give them sons to marry, **Ruth 1:11-13.** Ruth was loyal to Naomi; she had been with her for ten years. She witnessed Naomi's faith in God and became a believer.

So they traveled together and when they came to Bethlehem, Ruth asked Naomi if it would be ok to go into the fields and pick up the leftover grain so they could have some food. The Law required that the reapers leave some grain on the ground for *widows, orphans, and the poor.* **Leviticus 19:9; 23: 22.** *"When you reap the harvest of your land, do not reap to the very edges of your field, or gather the gleanings of your harvest. Do not go over your vineyard a second time or pick up the grapes that have fallen. Leave them for the poor and the foreigner. I am the Lord your God."* I love how even though the Israelites were God's chosen people, He cared and thought about foreigners! Foreigners generally worshipped all kinds of manmade gods. They didn't believe in the God of creation. In the old testament they were known as pagans where people didn't worship the God of creation, but they worshipped what God had created; like the sun, moon, and stars, or they made idols out of gold and prayed to them!

I'll be honest with you for a sec, when I first became a Christian, and began reading about how God chose the Israelites to be His chosen people and how he had the people that were known as pagans killed for various reasons. I just thought he did it because they weren't His chosen people. I wasn't looking at the whole picture here. I could only see my pain of the past and I was blaming God.

At that time in my life, I hadn't dealt with my issues concerning my childhood. I kept thinking, why! Why did you create me if you don't care about me? Why would you allow a defenseless, helpless child go through so much trauma?

I'll tell you right now, I was a very different person back then than I am today. Thank the Lord, that He was and is patient with me and my anger. I was blinded to the fact that He was there the whole time guiding me and providing for me in the form of people who fed and cared for me and my sister. It took years and a lot of help from the Holy Spirit to get me through such a terrible time in my life. When I finally figured it out, I was humbled and knew that even though He chose a small group of people to be His children, He was still thinking of me! **Galatians 3:14** says**, *He redeemed us in order that the blessing given to Abrahan might come to the gentiles through Christ Jesus.***

This is Paul speaking to the Galatians he told them in **verse 7-9 of chapter 3,** *Understand, then that those who have faith are children of Abraham. Scripture foresaw that God would justify the Gentiles by faith and announced the gospel in advance to Abraham: "All nations will be blessed through you." So those who rely on faith are blessed along with Abraham, the man of faith.*

So, the Lord thought of you and me, and if you look back, you'll see as I did that the Lord was and is providing for you. When Paul spoke of scripture he was referring to the only scripture they had, which was the Old Testament. We today have what is called the New Testament as well, which includes the gospels {*those that tell the story of Jesus*} and the epistles {*letters*}, which were written by His apostles including Paul to the various bodies of believers.

Some people think that the Old Testament is a Book that doesn't apply to us today. Friend let me tell you how wrong they are! As I study, rather it be a theme or a word study, it always takes me from the new to the old testament and back again. In **2 Timothy 3:14-17** Paul tells Timothy that he should continue in what he has learned and from whom he had learned it. In **verse 15-17** it says, ***And how from infancy you have known the Holy Scriptures, which are able to make you wise for salvation through faith in Christ Jesus. All Scripture is God-breathed and is useful for teaching, rebuking, correcting, and training in righteousness, so that the servant of God may be thoroughly equipped for every good work.***

Speaking of being equipped for good works, I married a wonderful, beautiful, and very patient man. We've known each other since we were kids. He is the baby in a family of eight. And I think he was his mother's *"baby"*. Well when I came into the picture it was not something she had envisioned for her boy. This lady hated me from the beginning. I believe it had to do with my family dynamics, which was so far from normal. His mother knew my mother was an alcoholic and she ran the bars. I'm only speculating, but I assume she saw my mother in me and decided I would turn out just like her. She would find every excuse in the world to keep her son away from me. We both worked at the local skating rink, so we would see each other all the time. We had been dating for about two years, when one day I came to his house to pick him up for school and found a note from his mother to him that explained if he would break up with me, she would buy him a brand-new car. I asked him about it, I forget the whole of the conversation, but he said no to her, and she wasn't happy about it at all. So my story is not like Naomi's and Ruth's where they loved one another and got along all the time. My mother- in-law seemed to do everything to make me miserable. But me being me I would try and do everything I could to please her because I loved her son. It felt almost like a competition between the two of us for her son's / my husband's affection. She would call and my husband would ask if I'd go pick her up and take her to the store. she loved to play bingo, and she wanted him to take her, so he made me go too. I was miserable. The back handed comments, and the dirty looks were hard to take sometimes. And that caused a rift between Bill and I. When our son was born everything seemed to change in the relationship. She would call and ask me if I'd like to go to lunch, or she needed to go to the store and she would be sure to tell me to bring our son too. She loved that boy. She would ask if he could stay with her while I worked sometimes. She began to spend a lot of time with us and would go on vacations with us. She and my aunt became friends, and they would share a room while on vacation with us and be sure our son was with them. When she became ill, I was the one to care for her and take her to her doctor appointments and such.

We ended up very close, The Lord got ahold of me and showed me that she needed love and compassion, and He used me to break her hard exterior, toward me. I was able to show her that I loved her son deeply and I would care for him always. She was one of those EGR people that I have mentioned in my previous books. *"Extra Grace Required."* Like I've said before, The Lord will put people in your face to show you how to love as He does. Trust me when I tell you, it's hard. I used to quote this Bible verse all the time before I came near my mother-in-law. **Philippians 4:13** says, ***"for I can do all things through Christ who gives me Strength."*** Paul of course was thanking the Philippians for sending him Gifts. They were concerned for him. He told them that he knew what is was like to be in need as well as to have plenty. He told them that *he had learned to be content in every circumstance, that he knew the secret, that it was only through faith in Christ that he was able to get through trying times.*

The Lord Jesus will, if you let Him, get you through as well. Remember reading scripture and praying is key to every situation. Oh, and taking deep breaths.

Speaking of taking deep breaths, I love to read scripture and one day years ago, I decided to witness to my two aunts. Well I'd ask them if they would be interested in studying the Bible with me, and they both said yes. So one day I took my Bible and went over to my aunt's apartment, and both were sitting there waiting for me. I helped myself to a cup of coffee and sat down and began reading. After a while I looked up from reading only to find that both ladies were asleep! That was the beginning and the end to my studying the word with my family.

My friend, that was the first time I felt the push or the stirring of my heart to teach the word to women. But I gave up. I allowed something so small as someone falling asleep to stop what God wanted me to do. Satan is really good at making you doubt your abilities to do what God says you can. He is a liar!

Remember Eve? The first woman to be created? Well Satan visited her and Adam in the garden and look what happened! She believed the lie! Satan asked Eve in verse one of Genesis chapter 3; *"Did God really say you must not eat the fruit from any of the trees in the garden?"* See how he worded it? He was twisting the words around to confused her. She told him; *"of course we may eat fruit from the trees in the garden," It's only the fruit from the tree of life in the middle of the garden that we are not allowed to eat," God said you must not eat it or even touch it; if you do you will die."*

In **Genesis 2:16-17** God was talking to Adam and put him in the garden and explain to him his duties. *The Lord God commanded the man, "you are free to eat from any tree in the garden; but you must not eat* *from the tree of the knowledge of good and evil, for when you eat from it you will certainly die."*

We must remember that God created Adam first and gave him instructions on how to care for His creation. Then God formed Eve out of the rib of Adam, so he'd have a mate suitable for him. I take it that Adam was showing Eve around the garden and showed her the tree that the Lord forbid him to eat. So Adam knew the cost, and he went ahead and followed along with his wife. **Chapter three of Genesis verse 6** says;

When the woman saw that the fruit of the tree was good for food and pleasing to the eye, and also desirable for gaining wisdom, she took some and ate it. She also gave some to her husband, who was with her, and he ate it.

Both of them sinned and now sin is on us all. But God didn't stop there, He forgave them and that was the beginning of salvation. Were there consequences? Yes! But remember it was a choice Eve and Adam made. God told Eve that in **Genesis 3:16** *"I will make your pains in childbearing very severe; with painful labor you will give birth to children. Your desire will be for your husband, and he will rule over you."*

They had it great! They had everything they needed to live a wonderful life within the presence of God and apparently it wasn't enough for them. after all was said and done, Adam and Eve realized they were naked, and it says that they made coverings for themselves... not each other now, they made them out of fig leaves.

This my friend is how we get it wrong so often. We tend to think too much and doubt what His plan is for us. The Bible says if we let the devil get a foothold in the doorway of our lives he'll come in and take over! It's up to you and I to keep the door of temptation closed! The Lord says to keep watch, be aware of it. When God is wanting to use you for His kingdom, be sure that Satan will do his best to try and stop it. We must remember that the devil cannot so anything without permission! We must Stand firm, and he will flee from us.

When Jesus began His ministry, He not only had twelve disciples but there were also women who chose to follow Him and in the book of **Luke chapter eight verses one through three,** it tells the story of how a few women who were so thankful for what Christ did for them, that they followed Him, and it says that they provided and supported the men out of their own means. Here you can picture the behind the scenes of Jesus' ministry. And how the women used what gifts they had and used them for the kingdom. They believed and didn't hesitate to act. I'm not like that. I have to think it through first and like some of the men that Jesus asked to follow Him, they had all kinds of excuses. but Mary of Magdelene and Joanna and Susanna as well as many others, chose to follow and serve Christ and not look back.

What is holding you back? Is it doubt? Or maybe you feel like I did, inadequate. Whatever the reason we need to pray and ask the Lord for help and guidance, and He'll give to you, just like He did me.

There is a great quote that says;

Most of the problems in life

are because of two reasons:

We act without thinking or

 we keep thinking without acting.

(Author unknown)

Ask yourself, what would you do if you were not afraid?

Food for Thought

1. If you had to describe your family dynamics in one word what word would you choose?

2. How does it compare or differ to that of Naomi and Ruth's relationship?

3. God will bring people into our lives, regardless of marital status, that we as believers must come face to face with and decide how best to show them unconditional love. AKA "EGR". Describe a time in your life when God brought such a person into your life. how did you handle it?

4. Ruth became a believer at some point in her interactions with her husband and his family. Is there someone in your life that is credited for you becoming a believer?

5. Faith is all about trusting in something you cannot hold in your hands; you cannot see it, and at times can be very challenging. Take a moment and describe a time when faith was all you had to rely on?

Notes

_____

_____

_____

_____

_____

_____

_____

_____

_____

_____

_____

"Sometimes you will never know the value of a moment until it becomes a memory"

Dr. Suess

Chapter 6

Tis the Reason for the Season

As I'm writing this, it is the Christmas season. I love seeing all the bright lights and homes decorated in reds and greens. It gives me a warm feeling, and I am always excited to go shopping to buy gifts for everyone. Living in Ohio I always wanted it to snow on Christmas eve. It rarely did it though. It would be cold, but it was mostly either dry or rainy, but on those rare occasions when it did snow I would go out when it became dark and just take it all in. I'd stand in the cold night air and take a deep breath in and look around me at all the lights people put on their homes and how their reflections made the snow on the ground glisten. I guess you could say I was in awe. I would stand there and just breath. I can't explain the feeling I had at that precise moment except to say I felt at peace.

It's funny how in the winter in the north all the leaves on the trees are gone. My children likes to call it "Stick Season" because it's so bleak. But I remember that it only lasts a few months and then in the spring we begin to see little signs of new growth. The grass turns green again and the leaves on the trees begin to bud and the flowers, oh my, the flowers. that were all dead become brand new and come up from the ground. I used to have Tulips, and I planted them in my front yard where I could enjoy them as I would sit on my front porch swing and enjoy my morning coffee. They never lasted long though and I'd plant other flowers later on after they quit blooming.

The point I'm trying to make is that things change all the time, we have to trust that change. Just like the seasons change we too can change and become new. In the Book of **Isaiah chapter 43:19** God was telling the Israelites His plans and He said: *"See, I am doing a new thing! Now it springs up; do you not perceive it? I am making a way in the wilderness and streams in the wasteland."* He was trying to give them a new hope, and the promise was fulfilled in Jesus' coming.

Now to understand the passage of what God was saying, you have to be able to imagine what the wilderness looked like in the Judean region. I've never been there, but I have been to the badlands in South Dakota. It is massive. The "free Dictionary put the definition of wilderness this way; *A wild, uncultivated, uninhabited region of forest or desert.*

It is vast and rugged, very little water if any, you cannot grow crops there. No one can live there and survive for long, no trees to shade you from the sun, nothing to keep you warm at night. But our God provided for them. In **Exodus 13:21-22** it says: *By day the Lord went ahead of them in a pillar of Cloud to guide them on their way and by night in a pillar of fire to give them* *light, so they could travel by day or night. Neither the pillar of cloud by day nor the pillar of fire by night left its place in front of the people.*

I could go down a rabbit hole with the whole cloud and fire thing, but I won't. I will say that God was making a point when it came to "gods", the gods of Egypt used fire and clouds as well. That's another study down the road. My point is that the God of creation provided for His children.

My next lady is the one everyone knows; her name is Mary, the mother of Jesus. What information I've been able to gather on the age of Mary is just speculation, but she was according to the traditions and customs of the time, around twelve to fourteen years old at the time of her betrothal. Can you imagine? What must that have been like for her, I mean she was a teenager!

She was more than likely thinking of her up-and-coming wedding and marriage and how to be a wife and then as she's minding her own business, in walks the Angel Gabriel! **Luke 1:28-38** tells the conversation that took place. Gabriel greets her by way of saying, in verse **twenty-eight**, *"Greetings you who are highly favored!"* it goes on to say that she was troubled at these words! This is from the NIV. The NLT says it best; verse **twenty-nine**, *Confused and disturbed, Mary tried to think what the angel could mean*. He goes on to tell her to not be afraid. That she had found favor in the eyes of God.

But my favorite part of the whole story, is in **verse 37** when Gabriel looks at Mary and says; *"For no word from God will ever fail."* This is after he tells her that her cousin, Elizabeth, who is old, will have a child as well. After the angel spoke to her and before he left, Mary had this to say, **verse 38** says, *"I am the Lord's servant, may your word to me be fulfilled."*

Remember I said that the old testament was what the people knew. Mary knew the Word and trusted in what the Angel had told her. **Isaiah 7:14** says *therefore the Lord Himself will give you a sign: The virgin will conceive and give birth to a son and will call him Immanuel. ("God with us")*

Isaiah 9:6-7 says *For to us a child is born, to us a son is given, and the government will be on His shoulders, and he will be called wonderful counselor, <u>Mighty God, Everlasting Father</u>, Prince of Peace. Of the greatness of His government and peace there will be no end. He will reign of David's throne and over his kingdom, establishing and upholding it with justice and righteousness from that time on and forever. The Zeal of the Lord Almighty will accomplish this.*

Trust. That is a word that is hard to do. It means *firm belief in the reliability, truth, ability, or strength of someone or something:* When I was a young believer and sitting in church service one Sunday, the pastor was preaching on that particular subject, and he like to always use object lessons in his sermons. I loved how he could break down a subject to show how the context in which the Bible uses the subject should be. He used on this day a chair to show how we as humans easily trust in the human aspect of things. He said whenever you pull out a chair and sit down in it, you don't stop and say wait a minute, do I trust this chair to hold me? Nor do we pick it up and examine it to see if it was made accurately. We just sit down. So then why do we have such a hard time believing in God the Creator and His goodness and trust Him at his word? We say we believe but we still refuse to trust.

Mary trusted what was told to her. Yea I know what you're going to say, *"If an angel stood in front of me I'd probably believe too."* Yea, I cannot argue with you there. But she knew the Word and trusted.

My favorite Christmas song is by Mark Lowry, and it is, to me, such a poignant reminder of what it must of felt like to be in her shoes.

Mary did you know
That your baby boy
Would one day walk on water?
Mary did you know
That your baby boy
Would save our sons and daughters?
Did you know
That your baby boy
Has come to make you new?

This child that you've delivered

Will soon deliver you

Mary did you know

That your baby boy

Would give sight to a blind man?

Mary did you know

Your baby boy

Would calm a storm with his hand?

Did you know

That your baby boy

Has walked where angels trod?

When your kiss your little baby

You've kissed the face of God

The blind will see

The deaf will hear

The dead will live again

The lame will leap

The dumb will speak

The praises of the lamb

Mary did you know

That your baby boy

Is the Lord of all creation?

Mary did you know

That your baby boy

Would one day rule the nations?

Did you know

That your baby boy

Is Heaven's perfect Lamb?

This sleeping child you're holding
Is the great I am.

That my friends is a great question "Mary, did you Know?"

We were chosen at such a time as this, just like Mary was chosen back then. He deliberately chose you and I at this time for His purpose! **1Peter 2:9** puts it this way; ***"But you are a chosen people, a royal priesthood, a holy nation, God's special possession, that you may declare the praises of Him who called you out of darkness into His wonderful light."***

We as children of God have the right to come to Him boldly and speak with Him personally. Jesus did that on the Cross for you and I. So now that we know the truth of the matter, let's take a deep breath and sit back and think about what God has in store for us. Once you know what you should be doing for the Lord, you know that special gift that you have? You can now begin your journey of discovering how special God thinks of you and showing others Jesus, by using that gift. You may not think of it as a gift but trust me it is. Think about what you are good at or what you like to do, and do it, to shine a light on Jesus. He's there with you just as He was with the Israelites.

In **Luke 11:33** Jesus was teaching on the light within, and he said; ***"No one lights a lamp and puts it in a place where it will be hidden, or under a bowl. Instead they put it on its stand, so that those who*** *come in may see the light."* We, my friends are called to be that light. So we need to let go of our troubling thoughts and self-doubts and get moving!

Mary, to me, is a great example of obedience to her calling. Even though she was young by today's standards, she listened to what the Angel told her, and she obeyed. She didn't doubt what was told to her. She said, *"I am the Lord's servant, May your word to me be fulfilled."* **Luke 1:38.** Now at the beginning of the conversation she did ask, **"How will this be since I am a virgin?"** She wondered but she didn't doubt what he angel told her. Unlike others in the Bible who were told they were going to have a child.

In **Genesis 18: 9-15** it talks of how the Lord appeared to Abraham and told him he and Sarah would have a child. *Sarah,* she laughed, I mean she was old! I'd probably laugh too. She laughed because of her disbelief or her doubting. **Verse 12** says, She laughed to herself, and thought, *"after I am worn out and my master is old, will I now have this pleasure?"*

The Lord asked Abraham why did Sarah laugh? and she came out of the tent and lied and said I didn't laugh, well the Lord looked at her and said, *"No but you did laugh." (NKJV).* But it doesn't end there, years goes by and no baby. Well Sarah being the woman we all can be sometimes. She took matters into her own hands. And told her husband to sleep with the servant so she could claim that child as her own. So he listened to his wife and a whole different set of problems arose for them. because of unbelief and doubting.

A whole nation was created out of Sarah's decision to take matters into her own hands. She was impatient, for one thing, and she thought she knew best and had her husband sleep with her slave named Hagar. Sarah didn't believe God. Have you ever asked for something only to think that the Lord was taking too long to answer, or maybe you thought He just decided not to answer at all? It's hard to wait for answers, I know. One of my favorite verses in the bible that I cling to when I feel that God taking too long is; **Jeremiah 29:11** which says, *"For I know the plans I have for you, declares the Lord, plans to prosper you and not to harm you, plans to give you hope and a future."*

But God's promises doesn't end there. He goes on to say that they would seek Him and when they did with **sincerity of heart,** then He would be found and He'd listen and bring them back from captivity, after seventy years. But He told them to prosper and live in peace where they were, and God would be with them. A pastor once said that we are to *"grow where you are planted"* it is up to us to be content where God puts us and learn to be happy in our circumstances and make the most of any situation. In other words be patient, and do not think you know better than the Lord.

At times, I have made the decision to take matters into my own hands. Trust me when I tell you that it never works out the way we want it to. Abram and Sarai They had trouble believing God when He told them his plans for them. The Israelites didn't believe God and look what happened to them.

Remember when God says it, it will happen, but in His time and not ours.

Then there is *Zechariah,* when approached by Gabriel, he said in verse **18 of Luke one,** *"How can I be sure of this? I am an old man, and my wife is well along in years."* You see the difference in the questions? *Mary wondered,* but *Zechariah doubted,* and because of his unbelief he was struck mute until the birth of his son. God still used him, but he had to suffer the consequences of his unbelief. Mary didn't know how, but she knew who to trust, she knew she was being called to serve God. Zechariah was the high priest, he was the one who went into the holy place to offer incense to God and prayed for the sins of the people.

He was considered a righteous man. **Luke 1: 6-7** says; *"Both of them were upright in the sight of God, observing all the Lord's commandments and regulations blamelessly. But they had no children, because Elizabeth was barren; and they were both well along in years."* I believe that she was not able to bear children because God wanted to show them that it is only by his grace and power that anything can be achieved.

I believe that If Elizabeth had had other children God's power wouldn't have necessarily been shown.

People need to know that the God of creation can and will achieve His purpose through us, but we must be willing.

Do you really want to be left out of witnessing His miracles? By doubting His goodness, and his promises? or His ability to accomplish what only God can do?

Food for thought

1. When the Christmas season is near, what are you thinking about?

2. Mary asked a question that I feel we can all relate to. "How can this be?"
   We all have asked that at one time or another, when faced with what we see as an immovable obstacle. Have you ever had an obstacle so big that it seemed impossible to move? Did you trust God to move it, or did you turn and try another way?

3. Think back to a time when there seemed to be no way out or no way through a situation and somehow a miracle was provided. Who or what did you attribute the answer to?

4. Have you ever considered what the process might look like, and how God would accomplish it?

5. Questioning God is ok. As long as we go to Him and talk to Him about it. Mary did. It's the way we ask that will reveal our faith. Take a moment and ask yourself, how I am approaching the Lord in prayer? Is it by faith or by doubting? Am I believing for my situation, or am I resign to the fact God will not answer?

Notes

"If God brings you to it, He
will bring you through it"

Rick Warren

Chapter 7

Jesus loves this hot mess!

The title to this chapter is one that explains a lot about me. I'm a hot mess! My daughter bought me a tee shirt that says so. I wear it often. I also have vinyl lettering on my kitchen wall that says; ***"all I need today, is a little bit of coffee and a whole lot of Jesus!"*** I put it there to remind me and others that Jesus loves me in spite of me. Also if I'm honest, I do like an occasional margherita. In my liquor cabinet , yea I said, "Liquor Cabinet" my daughter, again loves to shine a light on my faults, she bought me for Christmas one year a sign that says, ***"I love Jesus, but I drink a little"***. I keep it there to show people that I'm human and I am not perfect. A lot of non-believers think that if you're a "Christian" you are supposed to be. If I were to mention the things said to me over the years, I could write another book. If you've been a Christ follower for any length of time then you will know what I'm talking about.

People, regardless of who they are to you, no matter if it's a friend or relative, they will judge you based on your past. I know. Jesus knows my heart and knows that I'm a work in progress. Paul said it best in **2 Corinthians**

5:17, *"Therefore if anyone is in Christ, he is a new creation; the old has gone, the new has come!"* in **verse 16** Paul said we are to regard no one from a worldly point of view. Paul is telling us that the past is the past and we are not to look back and definitely not to judge someone based on their past. We are brand new on the inside, and it takes time to get rid of old habits. If we're reading scripture and praying and being honest with ourselves, then we will begin to change, and others will see the change. People who are closest to you are your worst critics. They will remind you often of your past. I have several family members who are good at that. No matter how hard I try to tell them that my past is in the past and I am not perfect, they continue to see me as being a hypocrite and Judgmental and that's not true at all.

I used to smoke; I quit in 1997 and I'm proud of that. I quit because I knew that the Lord didn't want *me* to smoke. It took a year to quit. Trust me when I say it was the hardest thing I ever did or will do! I'll never quit smoking again! I had bad habits and was changing before everyone and some of the ones I am closest to didn't like the change.

Paul reminded the **Thessalonians** in **verses 11 and 12 of chapter 4 of 1Thessalonians,** that they were to make it their *ambition to lead a quiet life,* to *mind their own business and to work* with their hands, so that their daily life may win the respect of "outsiders" and so they would not be dependent on anyone. And again in **Romans Chapter 12** Paul was teaching the people and urging them to behave like Christ followers. He says in verse 18:

"In as much as depends on you, live peaceably with all men". (NKJV)

It's all about changing to please the Lord, not men. I was trying to please the Lord and everyone around me, and I was failing miserably! I, like my *unbelieving* family and friends thought I had to be perfect, and I couldn't do it! The harder I tried the worst it got. As a new believer and not yet understanding that when you read the Bible you need to understand the *context* of which it is written. I read a Bible verse that terrified me. It says in **Matthew 5:43-48** Jesus was teaching about loving your enemies. He was explaining to them that we are to love everyone, not just our friends and family, but our enemies as well. Then in verse forty-eight He said; *"Be perfect, therefore, as your heavenly Father is perfect."*

He was speaking of our Character. In this life we cannot be flawless, but we can strive to be as much like Christ as possible. As a new Christian I didn't understand it that way. Not only was I trying to be perfect, but I was trying to make my family change right along with me. I was always telling my husband to stop cussing, and I would tell my son to turn the other cheek whenever he'd come home and tell me about some boys who were mean to him. That turned out to be a bullying situation that I didn't understand until my son began to shut down.

When I decided to come up for air as my aunt would say and get my head where it needed to be, I decided to investigate the matter and found that he was being bullied at the bus stop and at school. I took him to the bus stop one day and seen for myself what was happening. I tried to get on the bus and stop what was happening, but the driver would not allow me on the bus. So that was the day I decided that turning the other cheek was not something I was going to let continue. It changed my son, and it wasn't until he was in fourteen that he made the decision to defend himself. My son was and still can be the most generous of people. He would always give his stuff to people or buy them stuff if they didn't have money to buy whatever they may be selling at school. Kids took advantage of my son's generous nature, and I soon put a stop to that as well. I never gave him extra money to take to school anymore.

It is so hard as a young parent to know what to do sometimes, when it comes to our children. We want to defend them at all cost and protect them from the bullies of this world. Jesus said in **Matthew 23:37** *Jerusalem, Jerusalem, you who kill the prophets and stone those sent to you, how often I have longed to gather your children together, as a hen gathers her chicks under her wings, and you were not willing.* Jesus was saying that they were rejecting His help by rejecting Him. Just like my son rejected my help. I became a mother who hovered over her children and became over protective. I was told years later that they felt smothered.

Jesus too wants to protect us, but we must allow Him too. Me? I didn't trust enough to let Jesus take care of my son's situation. I tried it on my own and made a mess of it.

Jesus was concerned for the lost people and wanted them to know and trust Him and what He was telling them was true. Jesus would often go away by himself and pray. I can imagine the whole situation was quite frustrating for Him. No one seemed to understand His purpose. So he would go somewhere by himself and pray.

The first incident that I could find was when Jesus heard of the death of His cousin, John the Baptist. In **Matthew 14** Jesus had returned to His hometown and people were rejecting Him. They thought they knew Him. He was teaching in the Synagogue. When they heard him they said in the previous chapter and in verse **55**, *"Is this not the Carpenters son?"* meaning he wasn't *"Educated"* like the pharisees. They thought they knew him.

It is the same today people are so quick to judge you based on your external accomplishments or lack thereof. Jesus was told that John the Baptist had been killed and in **verse 13** it says, *When Jesus heard it, he departed from there by boat to a deserted place by himself.* Then along came over five thousand people and He fed them, and you know that took a while and then by the end of the day, He needed to go off and be by himself again. He could've been thinking about His family and how the ones closest to him didn't believe in Him or what He was accomplishing. We all have family members or close friends that are quick to judge us.

In **verses 22-23** of **Matthew 14** it says that Jesus sent his disciples across the lake ahead of Him and He sent the large crowd of people who were following Him away as well. He needed time by himself. Afterward He decided to catch up with the disciples and so the quickest way was to walk on the water. Did He want to help the disciples who were struggling against the waves? Yes! But in Mark chapter 6: 48 it says that Jesus would have passed by them, but when they saw Him and cried out to Him He stopped and helped. I think He wanted them, unlike his family members to believe in Him without the miracles. That is faith! Believing without seeing. But When He had neared the boat, the men thought they were seeing a ghost and cried out in fear. Jesus said to them in verse 27, *"Be of good cheer! It is I, do not be afraid."* Now Peter was the one to speak up and he said in **verse 28**, *"Lord, if it's really you, command me to come to you on the water."* And Jesus said, *"Come"* Peter hopped out of the boat and started walking to Jesus on top of the water, when he took his eyes off of Jesus and saw what I imagine he thought was impossible, he began to sink. See, Peter and the disciples were being tested to see where they were in their faith.

Reminds me of my trip to Alaska in which I had to fly to Seattle and then fly back, which was a five-in-a-half-hour flight. I think I have mentioned that I am terrified of flying! I get anxious and feel sick to my stomach and I have panic attacks! Crazy right? Well on the way home I decided I needed to be brave and trust the Lord to take care of the situation. Well let me tell you, the turbulence was all the way from Seattle to Florida! The whole way! It was like the storm with the disciples. He wanted me to trust Him in the storm, not only when things are going great. I have been told that I wrote my first book *"I Will Praise You in This Storm"* very well but did I read it? Yea I have read it, several times, and have had bible studies with it. Even as a "seasoned" Christian I still have my setbacks with doubting the Lord's goodness toward me. And I know the Scripture tell us to have faith and stop doubting that He cares for us and will take care of us. **John 10:11** Jesus said; *"I am the good Shepherd. The good Shepherd gives his life for his sheep."*

In **Deuteronomy 32** Moses wrote a song to the Israelites and recited it to the people. In **verse eleven** it says, *"like an eagle that stirs up its nest and hovers over its young, that spreads its wings to catch them and carries them aloft."* The Lord knows how frail we are and wants to guide us and protect us, but we must trust that He knows what He is doing! He knows we're not perfect, We are never going to be perfect until we are with Jesus! He loves us, not because of our accomplishments, nor because of who we are. We must trust Him and in Him alone.

Which brings me to our next lady, *the woman at the well.*

No one knows her name. The Bible does not say. She was a woman of mixed race. She was part Jew and part Assyrian. You can read the back story in **2 Kings chapter seventeen.** She wasn't considered "Pure", and the Jews hated them. Jesus however didn't live with such prejudices.

He was traveling through the region and came to the well that belonged to Jacob. Outside a town called Sychar in the region of Samaria. there Jesus sat and sent His disciples in to town to buy food, it was noon, and I imagine hot, and Jesus was tired. A woman came to draw water from the well and met Jesus there. Women didn't go out in the heat of the day to draw water; they generally went early morning or in the evening. But this particular lady did so, I think to avoid people and gossip. She had a reputation for liking men. She had been married five times and now was living with a man to whom she was not married to. In **John 4** Jesus sees the woman and asks, *"Will you give me a drink?"* the woman told Him *"You are a Jew, and I am a Samaritan, how can you ask me for a drink?"* You see, the Jews didn't associate with such people. **Verse ten** says; *Jesus answered her, "If you knew the gift of God and who it is that asks you for a drink, you would have asked him, and he would have given you living water."* She didn't get it. Which I can understand, it didn't make any since to her. Jesus was talking about water that can only satisfy the soul and not the body.

When as a young wife and mother, I was never satisfied with anything! I was always changing my house around, I Especially liked moving the furniture in my living room around, at least once a week. Bill would come home to find I had changed the furniture around. It aggravated him to no end. When I became a Christ follower and gave my life to Him, I began to change. It wasn't overnight or anything like that, but I became aware little by little that I was searching for satisfaction in the wrong places. No matter how many times I changed the living room around, I wasn't happy. I would also change Jobs frequently too. I just didn't know what was going on to make me so unhappy! I had a great life as an adult. I had a wonderful husband and a little girl who I adored. But something was missing, and it wasn't until Jesus found me that I began to change and see that the only thing that would ever satisfy me was letting go of my past and pursue my relationship with Jesus.

The living water that Jesus spoke about was the only thing that will satisfy us. He told her in **verse 13-14** *"Everyone who drinks this water will be thirsty again, but whoever drinks the water I give him will never thirst. Indeed, the water I give him will become in him a spring of water welling up to eternal life."* We are always searching for happiness. Someone once said, *"Happiness resides not in possessions, and not in gold, happiness dwells in the soul. This quote is by the Greek Philosopher, Democritus.*

That is what Jesus was trying to tell the woman at the well. She was searching for happiness in men. And she was never going to find it. Only Jesus can satisfy. I was searching for happiness in the way my home looked, but I never found it there, but I did find peace and happiness in my relationship with Jesus! I was then able to step back and see what true happiness and contentment is. Galatians 5:22-24 says it all.

But the fruit of the spirit is love, joy, peace, forbearance, kindness, goodness, faithfulness, gentleness, and self-control. Against such things there is no law. Those who belong to Christ Jesus have crucified the flesh with its passions and desires.

I've known people over the years that were always searching for happiness in material things. Thinking that it would make them happy. But it was only temporary. I know, I was one of them. not realizing that only Jesus could fill me. I had a friend years ago that always had to have name brand stuff. It had to be the best and she worked and worked to acquire it. She still wasn't happy. She was as they say, trying to keep up with the Joneses. It wasn't until she gave her life to Christ that she was able to let go of the material things and be happy with what she had. She, like me found what she was missing, a relationship with Christ! Living water.

Like me and my friend, the woman at the well, her life too changed the day she met Jesus, and she went back to town and told anyone that would listen about her experience with the Messiah. They listened to her and went for themselves and met the savior.

In **verses 28-30** it says; *Then leaving her water jar, the woman went back to the town and said to the people, "come, see a man who told me everything I ever did. Could this be the Christ?" They came out of town and made their way toward Him.*

The disciples brought the food to Jesus and told him to eat. Jesus told them that he had food that they knew nothing about. They didn't understand what He was saying. They thought someone had brought him physical food to eat. He told them in verse 34, *"My food is to do the will of him who sent me and to finish His work."*

You see, Jesus' message was, that we are to share the gospel that will satisfy the hunger that we all have within us! The woman at the well, her life was a hot mess! Jesus used her anyway! The people, after they went to see for themselves told the woman. verse 42, *"We no longer believe just because you said; now we have heard for ourselves, and we know that this man really is the Savior of the World."*

Jesus was trying to explain to the disciples about how the people were ready to hear some good news and how they were ready to believe but they needed someone to explain the Good news to them. They didn't get it. The woman with all her hot messiness did what she could to show people who Jesus was. That is what we are called to do as Christians. Like I said before, we don't have to be biblical scholars or anything we just need to be willing to be used. The woman was so excited, she didn't realize that she was an evangelist she just shared what Christ did for her. She was finally free to be happy!

I no longer change my living room around every week, and I was able to stay at the same Job for thirty years. Christ Changed my life, and I know He can do the same for you!

Happiness is a complex and subjective emotion. According to **Wikipedia**, *Happiness is a positive and pleasant emotion, ranging from contentment to intense joy. Moments of happiness may be triggered by positive life experiences or thoughts.*

I'm *learning* to find happiness or at least contentment in every situation. It doesn't mean that my life is perfect, nor absent of trials. But when the crazy happens in my life, I am *able* to recognize the fact that I need to stop, and take a breath, and know that Jesus is here with me, and He is going to handle it. I have to give it, whatever "IT" might be, to him though. **Matthew 11: 29-30** says, *"Take my yoke upon you and learn from me, for I am gentle and humble in heart, and you will find rest for your souls. For my yoke is easy and my burden is light."* My *NIV* footnotes defines His yoke as this, *"His yoke is the hard work and life's challenges of following him."* He doesn't promise us a life of ease when we choose to follow him, but He does promise to be with us. He promises us rest for our souls, and eternal life with Him.

Pastor Allen Jackson, whom I follow online puts it this way, *"He will give us the peace we will need to live with joy, in spite of our circumstances. He will fill us with the wisdom we need to carry out the plans He has for us."* We just need to be open and willing to let Him lead. That my friend is true happiness.

Food for thought

1. If you could have any life you wanted, what would it look like?

2. When do you feel the happiest?

3. What could you change in your life to bring you more contentment?

4. Money and possessions *cannot* bring true happiness, what if anything is keeping you from being truly happy?

5. Do you like to make others happy? If so, how do you do this?

Notes

"Only in God will you find
true happiness"

Author unknown

Chapter 8

Unsung Heros

I've known a lot of people over the years who were always working behind the scenes of the church. You never really hear much about them or what they are doing. When we attend a service we generally only see the Pastor, the Worship Leader, and band and that's what we tend to pay attention too. I love serving the Lord, but I don't want recognition. I get embarrassed so easily! I like to stay away from the spot light and serve the Lord quietly. If someone thanks me for something I've done, I don't know what to say, I mean I always felt that if I said thank you or got recognition for something, I felt it was being prideful on my part, and I wanted nothing to do with it.

As a young Christian, I read the Bible but didn't have a clue about context. In **Matthew chapter six verse one** it says, *"Be careful not to practice your righteousness in front of others to be seen by them. if you do, you will have no reward from your father in heaven."* Jesus was teaching about giving to the needy. He told them to not announce it with trumpets as the hypocrites do. He goes on to say that we are *not to let our left hand* *know what out right hand is doing. Our giving should be in secret. Then our father who sees in secret will reward us.*

That my friend is another one of those verses that scared me, and I made sure that whatever I did I kept it secret as best as I could. I spoke to a Pastor some years ago about it and he told me that I was being prideful by rejecting others appreciation.

Now that I have learned how to study the Bible using context, I know that Jesus was referring to people who were being insincere in giving or serving. We are not to do good for personal gain but with a sincere heart that wants to please God and not man, it should come naturally.

Whenever I read a passage such as the one in **Matthew chapter seven verses 21-23** that says, *"Not everyone who says to me, Lord, Lord, shall enter the kingdom of heaven, but he who does the will of my Father in heaven."(NKJV)*

The message here was to let people know that some of the so-called followers were using Jesus for selfish reasons and Jesus pointed it out. They were false teachers. There are still false teachers out there in churches; on T.V. we have to remember that the Bible is the true source and is trustworthy. We can take it at its word when we choose to study it, and not just sit back and let another human do the work for us.

The title of that passage is *"I never knew you"* these are the words of Jesus. They are part of what is known as the *"Beatitudes."* This word means *blessedness*. Which stems from the eight declarations by Jesus in **chapter five of Matthew** when He gave the sermon on the mount. They all begin with "Blessed are." These important instructions were given to *His followers* not to *unbelievers*. He wants us to think about what it means to follow Him and to know we're not alone. We must ask ourselves "Why" are we serving Jesus? Is it to please Him? Or is it to get recognition from the world?

I worked with a woman that would at times bring food from a food bank that needed to be eaten or would rot, to work and give it anyone who wanted it. She seen me and ask me if I wanted something, I said no, that I didn't do that. She took what I said as rejection. And she would be correct; I didn't explain to her that the refusal stemmed from a messed-up childhood that I was refusing to accept her generous offer, Even though She took my rejection personally, she was serving the Lord. I later explained the why of my rejection, after that I have learned to accept gifts.

As a child of an alcoholic and as the oldest of four I felt it was my responsibility to care for the other kids in the household. I was the oldest and wanted to make sure that me and my siblings ate. I would stand in a long line outside and wait for the doors to open at the salvation army that was giving away food, I would see the kids that I went to school with, and I was so embarrassed. I swore that as a grown-up I would do whatever I could to never take charity again. I never wanted to take it from someone who I felt needed more than I did, to me it was the same as stealing. My point is that I wasn't looking at the context of the situation and took what she was doing out of kindness the wrong way.

In **Acts Chapter 9** there is a woman that served others quietly and behind the scenes. Her name was *Dorcus*, and she was a lady who was a disciple of Jesus', and she loved to serve others. The Bible doesn't say a lot about her except that she became sick and died. And the mourners called for Peter to come to her memorial. She lived in the town of Joppa and in **Acts 9:36** it says, *In Joppa there was a disciple named Tabitha, {in Greek her name was Dorcus}. She was always doing good and helping the poor.*

She obviously made an impact on people because it says that she was always making robes and clothing for others and the widows wanted to be sure Peter knew who and what Dorus did to serve the Lord. She was a woman who used her talents to help others, especially the widows. She was kind and giving. She wasn't well known like Peter or Paul, but she was to those whom she helped. Peter was so impressed that he sent everyone out of the room and prayed over her and told her to get up. And she did! God obviously wasn't done with her yet.

Her faithfulness and her quiet servanthood helped to bring others to salvation. She never did it to impress people, she did it for Jesus, she did it because she cared for others. Like my friend at work who brought food to people from her church. Christ followers are called to serve. **1Peter 4:10** says, *"God has given each of you a* *gift from his great variety of spiritual gifts. Use them well to serve one another." (NLT)*

Colossians 3:23-24 says it best, *"Work willingly at whatever you do, as though you were working for the Lord rather than for people. <u>Remember</u> that the Lord will give you an inheritance as your reward and that the Master you are serving is Christ."*

Remember *all* believers are called to ministry, serving others is the very essence of the Christian faith. **Charles Swindoll** put it this way; *"Helped someone out lately? Take delight in forgetting the deed and being virtually unnoticed."*

Ephesians 2:8-10 says, *For it is by Grace you have been saved, through faith and this is not of yourselves, it is a gift of God not of works so no one can boast. For we are God's handiwork, created in Christ Jesus to do good works, which God prepared in advance for us to do.*

I met an elderly woman years ago who made quilts for our church ministry. I asked her what she did with them, and she told me that after each one is made she would tie many pieces yarn in the quilt to bind it and then say a prayer over each one of them and package it up for the church to give to either people in nursing homes or women's shelters. I thought that was the neatest thing and she said it kept her occupied. I could tell that she wasn't one to boast about what she was doing. I know in my heart that she was rewarded in heaven for it. She did it quietly just like Dorcus.

I remember seeing her at church when I was getting ready to give my "Cardboard" testimony, after I had taken a class on letting go of my past. A friend and I went to the storage room to pick out a piece of cardboard and there she sat at a table packing up her quilts. And me being me who love to chat with people and love meeting new people, began a conversation that was truly humbling, and I for the life of me cannot remember her name and that makes me a little sad, because she was unforgettable.

She sat there and in essence gave me her testimony. I know that the Lord brought us together so I could feel better about getting up on stage and telling the world my issues, and how with God's help I overcame them. she was a calm and beautiful woman whom the Lord knew I needed to hear from so I could know that I wasn't the only one in the world that had issues yet still be used to serve Him with the gifts He has given me.

I then was able to write down on that piece of cardboard what was before and what is now. On one side I had written *"broken and Shattered"* and on the other side I was able to write *"because of Jesus I am made whole."*

My point is that if we are filled with the past and junk that keeps us from serving Christ we are useless to Him. But once we let go of past hurts and all the junk that keeps us bogged down we then can serve the Lord sincerely.

My prayer for you is that if you are going through stuff, or something is keeping you from being able to serve the Lord, that you get on your knees and look to Christ for the answers. He will answer you and make you whole! But you have to take the first step. I did and I'll tell you my issues were crippling. But Christ came and changed my life!

Now that is not to say that my life became perfect, far from it! I still have moments of what they call PTSD, but I have learned how to deal with my issues and move forward in obedience to Christ.

I will stop and take a breath and pray and ask the Lord to help me and He does! We have to learn to lean on Jesus to get us through everything. My friend that takes courage, I know, but with the Holy Spirit's help we can and will succeed .

One of my favorite Christian writers said this about being used by God, *So many times we say that we can't serve God because we aren't whatever is needed. We're not talented enough or smart enough or whatever. But if you are in covenant with Jesus Christ, He is responsible for covering your weaknesses, for being your strength. He will give you His abilities for your disabilities!*

Kay Arthur

Patsy Clairmont who is my favorite *"Women of Faith"* Speaker wrote a book called ***God uses Cracked Pots***. I love how she used a piece of pottery that to you and I might be useless and should be thrown away, to express Just how much Jesus loves us. We're not perfect but still useable, we just need a little mending. Her testimony is awesome.

When I was a young believer and I thought everyone around me was perfect and as soon as I opened my mouth, they would know that I'm a fraud, I went to a Women of Faith Conference and when I heard the testimony of those women, I begin to tear up and realize that I'm ok! I may be a little cracked pot that set up on a shelf, but God got me down and mended me and is now using me for His good.

In the Book of **Ephesians** Paul talks of our *true Identity in Christ*. He had written to the Christians in the city of Ephesus to tell them of their role in the body and what the purpose of the church is all about. Remember *the church is a body of believers not a building*. It all started when the Holy Spirit came at Pentecost in Jerusalem.

Paul was instructing them as well as encouraging them to help one another and work together to help spread the Gospel. No one there was expected to be perfect.

Paul in **Chapter one verse three** of **Ephesians** said that we are *"blessed*, we are *Holy* and *blameless*, we are legally *adopted,* our *sins have been taken away*, we have the *Holy spirit* as proof that we belong to His family. He goes on to say in **chapter 2** that we are God's *handiwork*, that we were brought near to God, we are *no longer outsiders.*

Blessed in the Bible has several meanings depending on the context, Paul is not speaking of material things here in which we might think when we hear the word.

He is letting us know that as Gentiles we have been chosen and accepted as children of God. By Jesus' death on the cross, we too have been blessed with God's grace and mercy. We now can spend eternity with Jesus in Heaven! So with that said, we should want to do all we can to please Him. What a Gift! He thought of you and me!

Back in the nineties there was a song by *Brian Free & Assurance* called ***"He thought of me."*** A Beautiful song that reminds me that I was not nor ever will be alone. my favorite part of the song is this:

From the Garden where He prayed straight to Pilate's Hall

Where His perfect innocence took the blame for all

Then hanging on a rugged cross, though He spoke not a word

In Heaven, all over Heaven, my name was heard

Then I became the center of attention

I was weighing heavy on His heart

Though the soldiers tore His flesh in anger

I'm the one who tore His world apart

Way before He ever cried, "It's finished!"

Long before I ever bowed a knee

About the time He said, "Father, forgive them!"

Without a second thought, He thought of me

Way before He ever cried, "It's finished!"

Long before I ever bowed a knee

About the time He said, "Father, forgive them!"

Without a second thought, He thought of me!

Chapter Three of Ephesians says we can now *share in the promise of blessings* through Christ Jesus. I mean, before Christ's death on the cross only the high priest could get into the Holy of Holies, and he prayed for the Jews only, but now we as Gentiles *(Aka non-Jew)* can openly go to Him and talk to Him and have a relationship with Him and He'll listen! How awesome is that? **Chapter 4** discusses *grace* and how we have been given it *through faith*, God is rich in His *mercy* towards us, He has *equipped us for works of service*, what does that mean you might ask? Well we, you and I, have been gifted with special talents that we can and should use for the Lord and to help others to want to have a relationship with Christ. **Chapters 5** gives us instructions on how to behave as a believer and how *not* to put the Holy Spirit to shame. **Verse 15 of chapter 5** says, *Be careful how you live then, not as unwise but as wise, making the most of every opportunity because the days are evil.*

Chapter 6 is, I think, the most important of the entire book. In it Paul is stressing the importance of being strong and learning to stand against the one who will do everything possible to destroy our relationship with Jesus. He tells us to put on the whole armor of God. **Verses 16-17** says *In addition to this, take up the shield of faith, with which you can extinguish all the flaming arrows of the evil one. take the Helmet of Salvation and the sword of the Spirit, which is the word of God."* He has given us all the tools necessary to walk this life of faith, most importantly the *Holy Spirit* to help us in our weaknesses. He hasn't left us on our own. He promised to send a helper, and He did.

In **John Chapter 14** Jesus is explaining the only way to God. And that is by believing in Jesus and what he was about to do for them and us. He laid down His life for us, which means He chose to go to the cross for you and I. Nothing that had been done before had worked, so God made the decision to become the sacrifice for us. In **verses 15-18** He says to His disciples; *"If you love me, keep my commands. And I will ask the Father, and he will give you another advocate to help you forever- the Spirit of Truth. the world cannot accept Him, because it neither sees nor knows Him. But you know Him, for He lives with you and will be in you. I will not leave you as Orphans; I will come to you."* (NIV)

I hope and pray that you will allow God to take you down off that shelf and put you to use. Remember: *when the devil reminds you of your past, remind him of his future.*

Food for thought

1. Have you ever met a Dorcus? How did you feel after meeting them?

2. Describe a time when you were asked to serve in some capacity and resisted and Why?

3. Think about what you are good at. What gifts do you have and how might you use them for the Lord?

4. Have you ever felt like you could never be useful as a believer? Do you feel like a fraud?

5. What has changed in your life now that you are a believer?

Notes

_____

_____

_____

_____

_____

_____

_____

_____

_____

_____

_____

_____

"Leave a mark in this world
that will create a path straight
to Jesus."

Cathy Meyer

Chapter 9

I believe, Help my unbelief!

The title of this chapter comes from the book of **Mark chapter 9 verse 24**. In the NKJV. It is the story of how Jesus had just come down from the mountain where He was transfigured in front of Peter, John, and James, three of His closest friends. They came down to meet the other disciples and saw a great crowd whom the teachers of the law were arguing with. And Jesus asked them in **verse 16,** *"What are you arguing about?"* that's when Jesus meets the father of the boy who was demon possessed. The gentleman tried to explain the situation and said that when he had asked the disciples to heal his son, they could not. Now no one knows why they were not able to heal the boy, because in **chapter 6** they were able to when they were sent into the villages. Some speculate that they were only given permission for that day, or maybe their faith was wavering.

Jesus in **verse 19** says, *"O unbelieving generation, how long shall I stay with you? How long will I put up with you? Bring the boy to me."* It is such a cool story, because it says that when the spirit saw Jesus it immediately threw the boy into a convulsion. Jesus asked how long this had been going on, and the father said since he was a small child. Then in **verse 22** the father says, *"but if you can do anything, take pity on us and help us."* See where the doubt is? He didn't really believe anyone could help his son. He had asked Jesus to help him, but he didn't have faith. Jesus in **verses 23-24** says, *" If you can? Everything is possible for him who believes." Then the father exclaimed, "I do believe; help me overcome my unbelief!"*

Can you relate to the father? Boy, I can! I mean how many times have I prayed only to be thinking that it's not going to be answered, while I'm praying! I mean my doubts get in the way of my faith at times. The Holy Spirit knows this, and I imagine it makes Him sad. I have been going through some very private issues with a family member, and I pray all the time for the Lord's will to be done, but my thoughts are that His will may be something I don't want for them. that I want things to be done the way I want. I guess I want normal or what I perceive to be perfect. I know nothing in life, or anyone is perfect but if it could only be like the beavers in **leave it to beaver,** the show from the fifties and sixties that the family seemed so perfect. I never had anywhere close to that as a child. And I was hoping that as an adult it would be so ,because I was going to make sure it was so!

I have blamed myself for the issues, but I've learned that it doesn't help anyone. Not the family member nor me. I needed to go to the Lord with a quiet mind and an believing heart. My first book, titled *"I Will Praise You In This Storm"* is one that I wrote to help people to get through some of the toughest storms and how to do it.

During this trial I have felt like a fraud because I wasn't singing and praising the Lord during a very difficult time. My daughter said to me once, ***"Mom I know you wrote the book and I know you have taught the book, but did you read the book?"*** my child... I raised her right! She has become my mother! She was right though. I have read it and taught it and yes I wrote it. She was asking me if I believed what I wrote. That stopped me in my tracks, and as I sat there in my office, I began to pray and ask for the Lord to forgive me and my doubts and help me to rest in His promises and to learn to sit quietly and wait. I'm not quite sure when it happened, but Jesus must have seen my heart changing and now I am able to honestly say that I am trusting the Lord with my family member.

I think I've shared the fact that I love music, I listen to the words, one of my favorite singers is Jason Crabb, his song *"sometimes I cry"* is a beautiful song of how I feel at times and most Christians I imagine do too.it goes like this;

I look the part

Blend in with the rest of the church crowd

I know the routine

I could list all the bible studies in town

Watch Christian TV

I know all the preachers, their cliches

I've been born again

And without a doubt I know I'm saved

But sometimes I hurt and sometimes I cry

Sometimes I can't get it right

No matter how hard I seem to try

Sometimes I fall down

Stumble over my own disguise

I try to look strong

As the whole world looks on, but sometimes alone I cry

I try to speak faith

Never give that old devil, not even an inch to get in

I do worship and praise

Let everybody know just where I stand

On the back of my drive

Is a fish and a cross for the world to see

I know my God is good, all of the time

Yes, there's no doubt for me

But sometimes I hurt and sometimes I cry

Sometimes I can't get it right

No matter how hard I seem to try

Sometimes I fall down

Stumble over my own disguise

I try to look strong

As the whole world looks on, but sometimes alone I cry

Sometimes I fall down

Stumble over my own disguise

I try to look strong

As the whole world looks on, sometimes alone I cry

I try to look strong

As the whole world looks on, but sometimes alone I cry

"Sometimes I can't get it right, no matter how hard I seem to try". That's me in a nut shell. I love the Lord and know that I'm saved, but I keep hearing in the back of my mind Jesus' words to Peter; "O ye of little faith"

In the book of Matthew there are four different incidents that cause Jesus to say this to His disciples. **Matthew 6: 27-30** Jesus was speaking on worrying and explaining to them how He has provided for the birds of the air, the Lillies of the field. And yet they could not see that they were more precious to God than the birds or the flowers! In **Matthew 8** Jesus is coming down from the mountain and sees a large crowd and a man with leprosy comes to Jesus and kneels Down at His feet and says in **verse 2,** *"Lord if you are willing, you can make me clean." Jesus reached out his hand and touched the man. "I am willing," He said "be clean"*

The man knew he was not able to help himself; he needed Jesus! We're no different. He recognized the fact and made a move to seek help. In **Matthew 8: verses 5-10** is another story about a Roman Centurion who needed Jesus' help in healing his servant. He told Jesus that he knew he was unworthy of having Jesus in his home but if *he would just say the word* he knew his servant would be healed.

Jesus in verse 10 says, *"Truly I tell you; I have not found anyone in Israel with such great faith."*

When we doubt we are limiting our faith in God, When we have our minds set in a stubborn way or we have a strong opinion or belief. We have to stop putting up road blocks and relax and when we pray, pray the prayers of faith! It's all about trusting and learning to let go of self and giving up control to the one who can and will see to our every need.

Doubting is, after all, a part of human nature; I get that and know that it is hard for us humans to trust at times with things that are yet to be seen. We need to see it and touch it in order to trust something is real. But friend, the difference between people of faith who doubt, and people of the world is that we as Christians are and should be rooted deep in our faith in Jesus and what He has done for us. Yes, things are going to get crazy in this world and our lives will have bumps and bruises. But to successfully get through any crisis is to have genuine faith.

In **Jeremiah chapter twenty-nine** God, because of the disobedience of His Chosen, had allowed them to be taken captive. Here He was letting the Jews know what He was planning for them. they had been taken captive by the Babylonians, and God let them know that they would be there for seventy years, then He would rescue them. He said in **verse eleven through fifteen;** *"For I know the plans I have for you," declares the LORD, "plans to prosper you and not to harm you, plans to give you hope and a future. Then you will call on me and come and pray to me, and I will listen to you. You will seek me and find me when you seek me with all your heart. I will be found by you, declares the LORD, I bring you back from captivity."* God didn't abandon them He was always there. When we feel alone and forgotten, remember verse 11, He knows the plans He has for us! I repeat that verse sometimes whenever I'm in doubt and my life is crazy. God is always with me, and I know it. I sometimes get in my head and forget. But I am learning to not let the devil get a foot hold in my life, I merely close the door and begin to pray for guidance. The Holy Spirit is always there, ready to help and guide me in every situation.

I want to emphasize, that my doubts as a believer never ever were about God, who He is or if His word is true, but, I did and do sometimes fall back to the old stink'in think'in, where I began to wonder if I'm worthy of His goodness or If I'm worthy of His love. "Crazy Right?" The old self tends to creep in there and take hold. The devil loves to get in our heads and make us doubt rather or not we're worth the trouble. *The Bible is God's Word*, and we must believe it if we are to be successful in in our walk with the Lord.

***For God so loved the world, that He gave his one and only son, that whoever believes in Him shall not perish but have eternal life. For God did not send his son into the world to condemn the world, but to save the world through Him. Whoever believes in Him is not condemned.* John 3:16-18**

That my friends is such a great verse to memorize. That tells us that Jesus died for me! So that I could live! And that goes for you too! We must *believe* in our hearts not just our heads. You know by now I love music and whenever I listen to Christian radio, there is always a message for me in the words. One of my favorite songs is by **David Crowder, Dante Bowe and Maverick City** This song **"God Really Loves Us",** when I first heard it, I was blown away by how much I needed to hear those words at that moment, and how the Holy Spirit was there to remind me of the fact. He is so patient with me. Here are the words that I heard that day.

[Verse 1: Crowder]
I've got a friend
Closer than a brother
There is no judgement, oh, how He loves me
I've got a friend
And He is my strength
He is my portion
With me in the valley, with me in the fire
With me in the storm

[Pre-Chorus: Crowder]
Let all my life testify

[Chorus: Crowder]
Hallelujah
We are not alone
God really loves us
God really loves us
Hallelujah

Oh praise, my soul
God really loves us
God really loves us

[Verse 2: Dante Bowe]
His mercy's enough
His grace is sufficient
So come if You're needing forgiveness or healing
His mercy's enough
Oh, and this is our hope
The cross, it has spoken
Death is no more, Christ is the Lord
Oh, this is our hope, yeah
When I heard it, it gave me goosebumps. **God really loves us!**

When my husband and I moved to Florida after living fifty years in Ohio, it was an adjustment to say the least. Not just the weather, but the traffic and the crowds. But adjust we did. God provided a job for us right away, and friends.

I have two good friends that I've known for ten years, and we would hang out and go places and stay at the beach on occasion. We had so much fun! Life was great.

The Lord provided for us, especially me, because He knows that I need companionship and social interaction with others. He gave me that. Along with every other blessing I have and had over the years. God loves me, so why am I so hesitant at times to step out on faith and serve Him? His Word says that He will never leave me nor forsake me. As well as Jesus telling people to not worry. In Matthew 6:26-27 He said, *"Look at the birds of the air; they do not sow or reap or store away in barns, and yet your heavenly Father feeds them. Are you not much more valuable then they? Can any one of you by worrying add a single hour to your life?"*

I've found that worrying robs me of my happiness and most of all joy. I always would say of people who would upset me needlessly, "I'm not going to let that person steal my joy." I'm going to trust Jesus and His Word. But it's easier said than done, but try I do.

In **Matthew 14:31** again Jesus become frustrated with His disciples. He comes to them walking on the water, and Peter jumps out of the boat to greet Jesus and as he's walking on the water toward Him he takes his eyes off Jesus that is when he falters and begins to sink. Jesus asked him *"you of little faith" He said, "why did you doubt?"* I can imagine that Jesus was so frustrated at times with them, you can see it in the language He uses. We're no different today are we? I mean I for one was always Gung Ho at first to do whatever was asked of me then, I'd let my brain do a reality check and it said you cannot do that girl! We have to learn to re-new our brains to adjust to Jesus' way of thinking and not our human flesh.

In **Acts chapter twelve** we find a lady by the name of Mary, she was the mother of John Mark, who wrote the book of Mark. She was a prayer warrior. Peter sat in prison, and an Angel of the Lord came and rescued him. When Peter realized that it was of the Lord, it says in **verse 11,** *Then Peter came to himself and said, "now I know without a doubt that the Lord has sent His Angel and rescued me." Verse twelve* it says that *when this had dawned on him that he went to the house of Mary mother of Mark* he knew that people had gathered at her home to pray. When he got to the door the servant answered and when she saw who was at the door, she became so shocked that she closed the door on him and went to tell the others.

But they did not believe her. They told her in **verse 15** *"you are out of your mind!"* I wonder why? Was it because they didn't trust the servant? Or maybe their faith was lacking. They were praying but not believing. The prayer of the people were answered as they were praying but when the answer showed up at the door they would not believe it until they had seen it with their own eyes.

Isn't that just like us? Shame on us! I read the scriptures all the time and pray them, but sometimes I get into a situation where I feel that the Lord would answer for everyone but me. There, I confessed to my troubling thoughts and doubts, that sometimes creeps up. I still have those thoughts that I know Satan is putting there to tell me God really doesn't care about me, I'm not good enough. That comes from a messed-up childhood, and I need to remember that The Lord loves me and will always be here for me and will never walk out on me or give me away! That my friend is pride and pride is a sin! I'm a work in progress that was the old me and the new me knows better!

I know that it's not an excuse, I don't have an excuse. So I am praying that you and I together can get our life together and walk with Jesus honestly and faithfully.

Food for thought

1. Describe a time when you were fighting unbelief? How did it make you feel?

2. Do you recognize when the devil is lying to you?

3. Do you ever feel the need to act like everything's perfect in your life?

4. Do outsiders judge you because you are a "Christian"? how do you respond?

5. When praying do you find yourself not believing for the answer? Do you recognize the lack of faith? What can you do to change your "stink' in" think'in"?

Notes

Unbelief will block the channels of faith, it will rob you of joy, and, if undealt with, it will destroy you."

'John Bloom'

Chapter 10

Leading by example?

As a child in the seventies we played outside. We didn't have video games, nor were we allowed to stay in the house and get under foot as my aunt always said. One of my favorite games to play was *"Follow the Leader"*. We would choose a leader and then whatever the leader did we had to do the same. Anyone who didn't mimic the exact movement of the leader was out of the game.

Today as an adult, I've tried to live a life that my children could be proud of. I wanted to be a good example of what a godly life should be. I've tried to follow Jesus and live as he did, but I have not been able to mimic Christ as perfect as I would have liked. The great thing about following Jesus as the leader and not one of my childhood friends is that I'm never going to be out of the game, I'm never going to lose. I get a second chance over and over every day.

I took the kids to church; we prayed with each other. The thing is you cannot make your children do or be what you want, you can only lead by example and pray that they too will want to follow in your footsteps. My kids said that I was too much and was too preachy. I mean I get it;

I am not your quiet and meek type where people look at you and know they are either very shy or a Christian. I'm loud and bossy and want what I want and am not afraid to say it. Like my Bible study on the tongue? Yea that's me.

But I did my best. I love the Word and read it all the time and try to live out my faith in a way that would draw others to Jesus. At times I feel that I failed my kids, because neither one of them want anything to do with the Christian faith. In the book of **Proverbs chapter twenty-two verse six** it says, " *Train a child in the way he should go and even when he is old he will not turn from it.*" That is my hope. Or we can look at **Proverbs 13:24** which says, *"Whoever spares the rod hates their children, but the one who loves their children is careful to discipline them."*

I admit I was a strict parent and an overprotective one at that. I wanted to be sure that my children behaved in a way that would show others that they were well-behaved and good people. And they were and are! So I did something right. Right? I mean I didn't beat them or anything severe, but I did use the wooden spoons a lot. As adults, They even gave me a gag gift one year. They bought me a *"bouquet of wooden spoons"* for Mother's Day! One thing I was always proud of was the fact that I could take them anywhere and know how they would behave.

Which brings me to our next lady, or I should say ladies. *Lois and Eunice* from **2 Timothy.** To give a little back story, you have to know that a young man named

Timothy was an assistant to Paul. He was a young man that was taught by his Jewish mother, *Eunice* and Grandmother, *Lois*. His father was Greek and more than likely a non-believer. Timothy became a missionary and Pastor after Paul's first missionary journey. Then joined Paul shortly after for the next two missionary trips. Paul loved Timothy like a son. In **Philippians 2:20-22** , Paul describes him as someone who genuinely cares for people and takes an interest in them. He never thought of his own welfare but of those in need. I know that was because of his grandmother and mother who had a great influence on him.

They first heard the Gospel from Paul in the book of **Acts chapter 16,** where it says that Paul and Barnabas came to a town called Lystra while on his first missionary trip and it is believed that it was there that the ladies became believers and then taught Timothy about Christ and then he too became a believer. He not only became a believer, but he ended up becoming a Pastor.

You have to understand what these ladies were up against. The region where they lived was filled with people who worshipped gods like *Zeus and Hermes.* Zeus was thought to be ruler of the sky and weather. He also was considered the highest of the twelve Olympian gods. Hermes was Zeus's son and thought to be the messenger for his father. He was known as Mercury by the Romans.

When Paul saw a man crippled and healed him, the people assumed they were these gods. **Verse 11 of chapter 14** says, ***When the crowd saw what Paul had*** *done, they shouted in the Lycaonian language, "the gods have come down to us in human form!"* They were so excited they thought Paul to be Hermes because Paul was the one who did most of the talking. They were preparing to offer sacrifices to them, but Paul quickly put a stop to it. **Acts 14:14-15** says, *But when the apostles Barnabas and Paul heard of this, they tore their clothes and rushed out into the crowd, shouting: "Men why are you doing this? We too are only men, human like you. We are bringing you good news, telling you to turn from these worthless things to the living God, who made heaven and earth and sea and everything in them."*

When other Jews came and heard what was being said, they turned the crowd against Paul and Barnabas, and they stoned Paul, and thinking he was dead they dragged him outside the city and left him there to die. The disciples who believed came and helped him, then he and Barnabas left the next day. Did you hear that, **"He left the next day!** "Whoa! Talk about being criticized for your faith! He was beaten so badly that the people thought him to be dead. But God took care of Paul, and he was able to leave the very next day. Now I'm not saying he was completely healed, the Bible doesn't say. Even though all this took place I'd imagine in front of Lois and Eunice, they continued to believe and was willing to be different than the crowd and taught Timothy the same, now that's faith!

We as Christ followers are to do the same. We are to teach our children about Christ and His offer of salvation, as well as share the good news to others. Now I know it's unlikely that we would be stoned for sharing the good news to others or teaching our children here in the US. But there are places in this world that would in a heartbeat.

In **2 Timothy,** Paul begins his letter to Timothy by encouraging him to remain *faithful* and to try and not be discouraged. He says in **verse 5,** *"I have been reminded which first lived in your grandmother Lois and in your mother Eunice, and I am persuaded, now lives in you also."*

These special ladies lead by example. Paul reminded Timothy and encouraged him to stay the course, even though it was hard, and not to give up. Paul was another one who lead by example. Paul and the church at this time was experiencing great persecution, Paul was in a Roman Prison at the time he wrote this letter to Timothy. He wanted to encourage Tmothy that even though things looked bad, he was not to give up. In **2 Timothy 2:15** Paul said, *"do your best to present yourself as one approved, a workman who does not need to be ashamed and who correctly handles the word of truth."*

In order for us to lead by example we too must have that *steadfastness* that Paul speaks about. Steadfast means *"to be resolutely or dutifully firm and unwavering,"* We must remind ourselves and others that the Holy Spirit is here within us to help us stay strong, and to give us strength to not give up, when we feel intimidated by others who oppose the Christian faith. **2 Tim 2:7** says, ***For God did not give us a spirit of timidity, but a spirit of power, of love and of self-discipline.***

Timidity is a word that easily described me in my youth. It means *lacking in courage or self-confidence.* I was one of the most backward and shy child. I was afraid of everything; I know now that that comes from a childhood of chaos that was my life. I have, with the Holy Spirit's help been able to let that go and become bolder and more confident in my life and my walk with Jesus. Because of His love for me and His Word I can be *unwavering* in my faith.

We as Christ followers cannot possibly achieve this goal if we're not in the Word daily and if we're not trusting in the Holy Spirit to guide us as well as being taught the word correctly. We must be in a Bible believing church that preaches the truth. How will you know if they are preaching the truth?, Well, we must be in the Word daily! I cannot stress that enough. If you know God's word then you will be able to tell when someone is trying to deceive you, if we are ignorant of what God's instructions tell us, then we will be deceived.

The Word **deceive** means: *to cause to accept as true or valid what is false or invalid.*

To make someone believe something that is not true; to practice deceit.(Merriam Webster)

It's like when my husband and I bought our daughter a huge play house for Christmas one year. We wanted her to enjoy it right away and since it was winter in Ohio, we decided she could play in the house with it. "Mistake number 1". It took up most of the living room! So after all the gifts were opened, and everything was cleaned up we decided to begin putting it together. We didn't think we needed instructions at the beginning of the project, because everything was large and plastic and had very few parts, I mean what could go wrong? It had a roof, and four sides. One solid, "back" of house, two with windows, "sides", and one with a door, and a window "front" right? WRONG! It took forever and we finally realized that instructions would be a good thing. Once we read the instructions, it went together quickly. You had to put it together in a certain way, there was no, I think I'll do it this way instead. Nope, that didn't work.

It is the same with the Word and the Christian faith. God has given us instructions and if we follow them, we'll be able to lead a productive life and have that unspeakable Joy I spoke of earlier, as well as show others Christ, and not to be deceived into thinking we don't need to read the instructions.

In **Deuteronomy Chapter 11** God was giving the Israelites instructions for when they would cross over into the foreign land and about those who worshipped false gods. He was reminding them who the true God was, and they were to worship Him only. He also told them what would happen if they turned to the false gods. In **verse 22,** He told them; ***"If you carefully observe all these*** *commands I am giving you to follow- to love the Lord your God, to walk in all His ways and to <u>hold fast</u> to Him-."*

To **hold fast** means: *to remain tightly secured. To continue to believe in or adhere to an idea or principle:*

Psalm 119: 9-11 says, *How can a young man keep his way pure? By living according to your Word. I seek you with all my heart do not let me stray from your commands. I Have hidden your word in my heart that I might not sin against you.* This is one of my favorite verses in the Bible and one of the first ones I memorized as a young believer. I prayed these passages over and over. It not only helped me to memorize scripture but as a young believer, I was learning how to pray and speak with the Lord.

Oswald Chambers said it best, *"We have to pray with our eyes on God, not on our difficulties."* That is so hard to do if we are not totally focused on Him at the time of prayer. Most of the time, when we do go to the Lord, it is during a time of great hardships or something traumatic happening in our lives.

At this particular juncture in our lives, My husband and I have been at a crossroad as what to do about retiring and either staying in Florida or moving back to Ohio. We've struggled with this issue for a year or so. My husband's health being the main reason for such a decision. Living in Florida is a costly adventure and with him needing to quit working and losing all that money, it was decided that we needed to downsize. So we were doing everything we could think of to stay in Florida. Well not long-ago God took the decision out of our hands and took care of it for us. Bill was no longer working and with everything about his health, the decision was made to go back home and be closer to our daughter. I thank the Lord each and every day for making the choice for us. We struggled so much because we love our lives here and our friends, our church, I mean, we were content until we weren't. you see I took it upon myself to be in charge and try to make decisions without the Lord's input. I was a hot mess! The only thing that was on my mind was how much money we would be losing, and we would no longer be able to afford the lifestyle that I grew accustomed to. That being said, Bill and I as a young married couple, struggled to make ends meet for years. Now we no longer had to use a calculator when going to the store. I could go shopping at the department store and not worry about the cost, and I was able to drive a brand-new car and not worry about it breaking down, and if it did we could afford to get it fix.

When Bill's job came into question, I was being selfish and thought if only He could work another year. I wasn't thinking of my husband and his health, I was thinking of our lifestyle. At times I would pray and ask the Lord what to do, but each and every time the answer was in front of me, I ignored it. Sometimes I wanted to Lord to knock on my front door and come in and sit down and say: **"Ok, this is what we're going to do."** But then I could tell him what I wanted and try and explain the situation so He would see my point of view. Wouldn't that be awesome?

Praying to the Lord is easy. But there is *a right way and a wrong way*. I know.

Psalm 119:36-37 says ***Turn my heart toward your statues and not toward selfish gain. Turn my eyes away from worthless things; preserve my life according to your word.***

He is listening and if we as His children just pay closer attention, then we will hear from Him. He was always telling me to listen! Like I tell the kids on the bus, you can't listen if you're doing all the talking. Well, Cathy was doing all the talking. I guess if I'm honest, I knew what He wanted and what My Husband needed to do. But I wasn't ready for that. I liked my life here. But God said no. I was afraid of what He was doing in our lives and not trusting Him to take care of the situation.

In the book of **Isaiah 43:19** it says; ***He will make a way where there is no way. "Behold I am doing a new thing; now it springs forth, do you not perceive it? I will make a way in the wilderness and rivers in the desert.'***

We must learn to stop and take a breath and relax enough to focus our attention on the one who will listen without distractions. And not on our issues. He will listen to us and hear us even when we're selfish. He knows what is best and just wants to hear from us. Remember that the Holy Spirit goes to the Lord with our request.

(Romans 8:26-28). ***In the same way, the Spirit helps us in our weakness. We do not know what we***

ought to pray for, but the Spirit himself intercedes for us through wordless groans. And He who searches the hearts knows the mind of the Spirit because the Spirit intercedes for God's people in accordance with the will of God.

Remember, prayer is just talking to the Lord as to a friend. A friend doesn't expect you to have fancy words when communicating with them, neither does the Lord.

Food for Thought

1. Do you recall a special person in your life that lead a faithful life and taught you the same? Do you contribute your faith to them?

2. What does leading by faith look like to you?

3. What challenges might you face when leading by faith? How can you overcome them?

4. Do you remember a time in which you prayed selfishly? What

   Was it, and how did God answer?

5. What are some ways you as a believer, can be intentional when it comes to leading others to Christ?

Notes

"A Leader is one that knows
the way, goes the way, and
shows the way"

John C. Maxwell

About the Author

Cathy Meyer has written two other Bible studies "I will praise you in this Storm" and "Shut My Mouth O'Lord". She loves the Word and teaching it to others. She lives with her husband of over forty years and their two cats, Sammy and Chloe.

She is, like everyone, trying to find her way in this world while still being committed to Christ. Her desire is to help others learn to walk with Jesus and learn to feel comfortable in their own skin, even though they make mistakes. To know God still loves them and they, like her, can start fresh each and every day.

You can find her books on amazon; or e-mail at cm.biblestudybooks@gmail.com

www.ingramcontent.com/pod-product-compliance
Lightning Source LLC
Chambersburg PA
CBHW071945170626
46813CB00005B/1831